STRANGERS LIKE US

MARY CAMPISI

MARY CAMPISI BOOKS, LLC

INTRODUCTION

Readers who loved Mary Campisi's bestselling Truth in Lies series also known as the "A Family Affair" books, won't want to miss *Strangers Like Us*, Book One in Mary's new Reunion Gap series.

Yes, there's heartache, betrayal, forgiveness, redemption, and second chances. But…this small town doesn't open its arms to strangers and wayward drifters. Why? Because years ago, many of the residents were swindled out of their life savings by the smooth-talking stranger they trusted.

So, what happens when a beautiful woman arrives in Reunion Gap, bent on helping the town and those in need? Well, a person can only fight the laws of attraction so long…and good deeds should not go unnoticed, should they?

When the son of the man who lost everything falls in love with the daughter of the man who stole it all, there can only be heartache ahead when she's exposed. And she *will* be exposed. It's only a matter of time, and no matter how good her intentions, heartache is coming.

Will forgiveness and redemption follow?

Stay tuned! It's going to get very interesting.

And for *A Family Affair* fans, remember the private investigator Lester Conroy? He's promised Mimi Pendergrass he'll find out what happened to her daughter. Guess what? The trail leads him to Reunion Gap!

Reunion Gap series:
   Book 1: *Strangers Like Us*
   Book 2: *Liars Like Us*
   Book 3: *Lovers Like Us*
   More to come!

Print ISBN: 978-1-942158-38-7

LETTER TO READERS

Dear Readers:

Welcome to the Reunion Gap series. I'm so glad you've decided to join me as we head to the small town of Reunion Gap, Pennsylvania. If you've read my work before, you know I love writing about hope and second chances in small towns where the residents have known their share of heartache and betrayal. I grew up in a small town in northwestern Pennsylvania, so it feels very natural for me to write about a place where everybody knows everybody and a handshake is your word.

And I know all about close families and sibling dynamics and that blasted pecking order! (Can you tell I'm a middle child?) But I also know about sticking together, and that while my brothers and sister and I live hundreds of miles away from that little town in Pennsylvania, it is still part of us—it will always be part of us—because that's where we learned the true meaning of family and friendship, and the importance of honoring your word.

Enjoy!

Mary

To Brenda: a woman of courage, strength, and resilience.
Godspeed!

1

Rogan Donovan once believed in the power of possibility and the beauty of a dream. But that was before a stranger came to town and ripped a hole in his father's good name, shredded the man's self-respect, and left him with nothing but a mountain of debt and a guilt so deep it could only be relieved through a bottle. It was the bottle that became his constant companion and possibly, his ultimate demise.

Rogan poured a whiskey, tossed it back, and stared at the grayness of the pre-dusk sky. The May breeze lifted the edges of the financial reports he'd been reading. In another life, he would not be sitting in a rocker on the front porch of a rundown farmhouse at the edge of town. He'd be married with a child, living the dream life he and his fiancée had mapped out. They'd spent many a night enjoying the view from their penthouse as they sipped Chardonnay and talked about the magnificent future they'd share.

That future was gone, along with the dreams and the fiancée, strangled by the phone call from his mother two years ago. *Oh, Rogan, something horrible's happened.* She'd cried so hard she couldn't get the words out. But his sister could. That was one thing about Charlotte; she was never at a loss for words. *Dad's gone and lost everything, Rogan. Everything that's ever mattered to him and Mom, including their reputation. Now what's going to happen? What are they going to do? Huh? They're almost broke. You have to help them. Somehow, you have to figure a way out of this mess. Please, Rogan, you're the only one who can.*

"Two pennies for your thoughts."

He hadn't heard the screen door open or his uncle's six-foot-three frame slide into the rocker next to his. Rogan turned, shrugged. "No thoughts, just enjoying the quiet."

Oliver Donovan shook his head, his gray ponytail bobbing with the action. "You feed that BS to somebody who doesn't know you." He crossed a booted foot over his thigh, rubbed his jaw. "I know where that brain of yours is going. It must be down-right exhausting to rescue people from their own mistakes, even if they don't want to be rescued. Don't you ever take time off?" His deep voice shifted. "Have a little fun with one of those young ladies who've been asking about you? Hallie or Leah?"

Hallie Richards wanted a commitment, and word had it, Leah Boardman wanted a baby, not necessarily, the man who went with it. "Uh, no thanks." Besides, after Deborah broke their engagement, he'd decided the no-strings, casual approach was the way to go. Enter Alyssa. They met up every Thursday, discussed the latest stock trends, and then enjoyed each other's bodies and a bottle of Merlot. Nice and neat. No strings. No expectations. No chance to get hurt again.

Just the way he liked it.

"You ever going to get past that girl who dumped you?" Oliver's words grabbed him around the throat, squeezed. "The way I see it, you're hanging onto a dead end. If the woman you'd planned to spend the rest of your life with couldn't understand why you came home, maybe even admire you for it, she might have been the wrong one for you. Did you ever consider that?"

No, he hadn't considered the brilliant brunette with the long legs and witty sense of humor was wrong for him. In fact, she'd been exactly right up until he told her he had to take a leave of absence from his job and head back to Pennsylvania to help his family. Deborah hadn't liked the sound of that, especially the part about leaving Los Angeles and heading to a small town. But once she found out money was involved, as in a disastrous situation that had flattened his parents and left his father in a semi-stupor? Well, that was a little too much emotion for her, and worse, she wasn't ready to take on his family's debt or their time requirements. *Too messy*, she'd told him. *Too complicated, and nothing personal, but I didn't sign up for life in the boonies and the parent bailout program*. She'd returned his ring with a kiss on the cheek and a wistful smile. *Call me if your situation changes, and maybe we can discuss things.*

That was the last time he'd heard from his ex-fiancée, though one of his buddies told him that six months later she moved in with a stockbroker pulling down seven figures a year.

"Rogan? You still dreaming about the West Coast?" His uncle's voice gentled. "Maybe you should close that chapter and think about settling down, find a wife, have a kid."

Rogan tossed his uncle a look that, even without words, could be interpreted as *not happening*. He ignored the question and asked one of his own. "I could say the same to you. Did you ever think about finding a wife and having a kid?"

That made his uncle laugh. "Never entered my brain, not in fifty years." Another laugh. "Besides, I'm not about to start sharing a bathroom or the remote control with anybody."

The last laugh held a hint of what sounded an awful lot like regret. Did his uncle wish there *had* been a woman and a child in his life? If Oliver Donovan wanted either, it was hard to believe he couldn't have had them. The man was a mix of mystery, musician, and philosopher, with a live-and-let-live attitude who played a mean keyboard. Women in their twenties all the way to their seventies stopped by his music shop to hear about the time he spent touring with his band, playing keyboard and writing music. He had a collection of vinyl records in a temperature-controlled room, and he played them every Wednesday and Friday from 3:00 p.m. to 7:00 p.m. Passersby stopped to listen, no matter their age or music preference, and Oliver welcomed them into the shop, told them a story, made them feel like they belonged. Money had come and gone in his life, but Uncle Oliver, who preferred to be called "Oliver," was never owned by the gain or loss of it. Maybe that's why he didn't "disown" his oldest brother, when Jonathan miscalculated the sincerity of a stranger and lost a chunk of his money.

"You talked to your aunt lately?"

Camille Alexander, the aunt who'd once declared that not all Alexanders were lying, cheating connivers and married one to prove it, found out before her first anniversary that, while some might be trustworthy, her husband was not. The desire for money and power had blinded her to Carter Alexander's philandering ways and though she threatened divorce at least once a month, no one believed it would ever happen. Camille would rather be miserable than broke, *broke* being a relative term for someone who'd grown accustomed to caviar and private planes. "I heard she was in New York." Rogan paused, added, "Again."

"Of course she'd be flitting around instead of trying to figure out what she's going to do with the rest of her life." A long sigh, followed by an even longer one. "At some point, a person's got to stop hiding behind designer duds and past hurts and take responsibility for what happens next."

"Yup." Rogan reached for the bottle of whiskey, poured another glass.

"Better watch that stuff. It's taken down more than one Donovan."

4

Oliver meant his brother, Jonathan, Rogan's father, who'd died last year from an eighty-foot fall off Shadyside Rocks. Nobody needed to review a blood alcohol test to figure out he'd been drinking. The man had barely seen a sober day since the scam that ruined his life. The real question that had no answer was whether the fall was an accident or intentional. Rogan's father wasn't the only one who'd had his troubles with the bottle. Oliver had a scare a while back, but since the night he refused to talk about, the former "sex-drugs-and–rock-n'-roller" had cut the drugs, including alcohol, from his go-to list. Now, he drank straight-up water, grew herbs and vegetables in his back yard, and advocated recycling, composting, and repurposing. The man still wore a ponytail and earring, sported tattoos from his younger days, and he'd never give up his rocker T-shirts, but life these days was more about compassion, clean living, and the environment. "You think Camille went to New York to hire a lawyer?"

"For what? To talk about the divorce she's never going to get?"

Rogan sipped his drink, shrugged. "Maybe. I mean, why would you stay married to a serial cheater?"

"Why?" His uncle slid him a look that said he still had a lot to learn about human behavior. "The guy's a doctor, *and* he's an Alexander."

"Yeah, well, not everybody wants to be an Alexander." His father had always said that name was synonymous with liar and cheat. Rogan had gone to school with a few of them, and the description was dead on, except for Tate Alexander. He'd been a decent guy who got caught up in his family's dysfunction. Rogan hadn't heard about him since Tate left town six years ago, the same day as his mother's funeral. Talk about strange and full of secrets...

"Your aunt's messed up," Oliver said.

"You think she still loves him?" Now *that* would be messed up.

Oliver nodded. "Sad but true. I've seen the way she talks about him, one part cussing him up and down, and the other hiding the hurt." He rubbed his jaw, reached for his water. "Who needs that?"

"Exactly."

"Hey, I'm not saying you shouldn't try for the happily-ever-after. You might get it right, who knows? Your parents had it figured out—" he paused, his voice dipped "—for a while."

Yeah, right up until Gordon T. Haywood walked into Reunion Gap with his promises to fill Jonathan Donovan's empty building with men and machines to reopen the plant. This month marked the second anniversary of the disaster that ruined lives, including his father's. But Gordon T. Haywood stole a hell of a lot more than money: he stole his father's hope. A man without hope is no better than a ghost, afraid to breathe, determined not to trust again, bent on blaming somebody for his misery, usually himself. Curious that the Alexanders stepped in and bailed out a select number of families who'd invested in the factory's reopening by paying off their loans and making them "whole." That caused its own pain, made the unchosen ones furious, and then it made them desperate.

"You're thinking again, and it's not about balance sheets or month-end analysis." Oliver pierced his thoughts, pulled him back. "I know what this is about. You've got to let it go, Rogan. Two years is a long time to do penance for a sin you didn't commit."

Rogan sipped his whiskey, avoided his uncle's too-knowing gaze. "No idea what you're talking about."

"Right. Then let me spell it out for you again, like I've been doing since you came home. What happened to this town isn't your fault. It wasn't your father's fault either. The only sin he ever committed was trusting people too much. The one to blame is the bastard who came to our town and stole from us. Should we have made him take a lie detector test to prove his honesty? We were all ripe for the picking and he knew it. The guy probably homed in on towns like Reunion Gap, knew we were desperate for a chance to turn things around. He played all of us, with more skill than Donnie on vocals."

Donnie being the lead singer in Oliver's old band.

"That's not the point."

"Sure it is, but you don't care, do you? You're hell-bent on trying to fix everyone's misery, loading it on your back, or your computer, so they stop blaming your old man. Well, you know what? I lost money, too, and I don't blame him. I never blamed him."

"That's because you're his brother."

"It's because I'm an adult who made the decision on my own. Your dad didn't force me to do anything, and since when did you ever know him to be the persuasive type? Huh?" His voice grew stronger, filled with conviction. "I'll tell you. Never."

"People trusted him. That's why they invested their money in a business Haywood never intended to bring to this town. Didn't matter the business didn't exist; my father made people believe it did because *he* believed it did. And look what happened. I'm going to do everything I can to help the people who lost out because of it."

"For how long? Ten years? Twenty?"

"I don't know." Pause. "I just don't know."

"Your father never wanted you to come back here. Neither did your mother. They wanted you to live your life and not worry about them."

"I couldn't do that." After his sister's near-hysterical phone call begging him to come home, he knew he had to find a way to help his parents. People blamed Jonathan Donovan for their misfortunes, but what they didn't know was that Rogan was just as much to blame. If he'd listened to his father's request to review Haywood's proposal, maybe this could have all been prevented. Maybe his father would still be alive. But he'd ignored him, made ten different excuses why he didn't have time to review the documents and give his opinion. And why was that? Oh, right. He and Deborah had been about to embark on an Alaskan cruise. It didn't matter that Rogan was an accountant with a gift for finding inconsistencies, or that his father wouldn't recognize an ill intention if it stood next to him. Deborah wanted to go to Alaska, see the glaciers…

So, they'd gone and his father made the biggest mistake of his life. But so had Rogan. He'd never told anyone what he'd done, or rather, what he *hadn't* done, not even his uncle.

The pain was too deep.

If Rogan had looked at the documents and asked a few questions, he might have saved his father and the town from a lot of misery. But he hadn't, and his selfishness had been his father's undoing.

He would not be selfish again.

No matter what.

ELIZABETH HAYES KNEW what it meant to be alone, knew the difference between alone and lonely. She'd been both for much of her life. There'd been no siblings, no close friends, no pets, just her mother, her father, and Everett Broderick, a man she called uncle who was no blood relation. Uncle Everett was her father's business partner and had been part of their lives for as long as she could remember. It was Uncle Everett who taught her to swim, play chess, and compose a proper photograph. He'd also shown her the difference between trying and commitment, and the importance of an apology. She'd stopped wondering years ago why her parents weren't the ones bestowing the lessons. Weren't mothers and fathers supposed to teach their children about responsibility, good citizenship, right from wrong?

Weren't they supposed to be role models?

Her solitary lifestyle led her to contemplate nature, the gentle swaying of a fern reaching skyward, the layers of a bird's nest woven in a most intricate design, the glitter of fresh-fallen snow. These observations took her on walks in the park, hikes in the woods, and sloshing in streams. She began drawing what she saw, gathering flowers and leaves to study their patterns and press them between thick books. How could she know this obsession with nature that brought her such peace would grow into a career?

At age twelve, she learned the greatest life lesson of all from her parents: the fanciest words spoken in the most compelling manner did not make them true. Her parents *wanted* to be all things to her. They wanted to teach and guide her through their own actions, but they did not possess the internal strength to do so. They weren't models to be used as examples unless one were interested in material gains without regard to right or reason. Where was the compassion for the less fortunate? Why did her mother not volunteer at the food bank or the shelter, or at the very least donate last season's clothes since she refused to wear them again? Why did she feel it necessary to hand them over to thrift shops to be sold? They had so much when others had so little, and yet, they acted as though what they had was not enough—would *never* be enough.

Elizabeth decided long ago this would not be her life. She would not be controlled or manipulated by *things*.

All she wanted was her parents' love.

Was that really so much to ask?

Apparently so.

Elizabeth might have been better prepared to accept her

parents' faults if they hadn't been so consumed with each other that they'd excluded *her* from their intimate circle. Oh, they loved her in their own distracted way. They dressed her in designer fashions, surrounded her with exquisite beauty, and sent her to the finest schools. Hadn't she traveled to London and Rome before she was thirteen? But she was never part of the *reason* they existed, never the air and breath that some parents claimed. Phillip and Sandra Hayes breathed and lived for each other, and there was simply not enough oxygen left for their daughter, and now they were both gone, taking the mystique of their existence with them.

"I know how much you miss your parents, and I know it's not the same, but I'll always be here for you."

She met Uncle Everett's kind gaze, forced a smile. He was all she had left now, the closest person to a relative, and he wasn't even related. What did that say about her? Was she unlovable? Or was she simply unable to love? "Thank you." Twenty-eight days ago, the small-engine plane crash had taken her parents without warning. No goodbyes. No final, tepid *I love you*s.

Uncle Everett cleared his throat, turned toward her. "They did love one another immensely." He adjusted his horn-rimmed glasses, blinked. "And that was both a blessing and a curse for those who had to witness it. Such devotion for another person is a true testament of a powerful love that burns so bright it scorches those who try to draw close."

The man loved poetic commentary, especially when it had to do with a lesson or an observation. Such as now. She might not be a true relation to Everett Broderick, but she possessed the same intuitive ability to interpret a feeling or a situation that others might miss. It was a gift that sometimes caused as much misery as joy. What child wanted to acknowledge that her own parents needed one another more than their only child?

That knowledge left scars so deep, they bred feelings of inade-

quacy and self-doubt and resulted in disastrous, ill-fated relationships.

After the last mess that ended in a three-hour rant in which her
soon-to-be ex accused her of an inability to commit or trust—just
because she refused to move in with him—Elizabeth decided men
were too much trouble, and for the foreseeable future, she'd
choose the single state. It should have bothered her that she could
toss aside a man she'd dated for six months and shared a bed with
for four, but it didn't. She'd been happy enough and liked his
company, but to move in with him, see him every night and every
morning? Have him in her personal space, expecting he had a
right to be there? No, that was not what she wanted, and it was
better he find out now. Last she heard, he'd started seeing his
yoga instructor and they were moving in together. Again, why no
twinge of jealousy, no spurt of anger that she'd been so easily
replaced?

What was missing in her DNA? *What was wrong with her?*
Why didn't she have feelings like normal people?

"Elizabeth?"

When Everett Broderick said her name that way, she knew it
was about more than getting her attention. He had a message, a
big one, and he wanted to make sure she heard it. "Yes?"

"Your father and I worked together a long time." His soft
brown eyes misted beneath the horn-rimmed glasses, his shoulders slumped. "But—" he paused, licked his thin lips "—there are
some things that happened along the way that changed us, especially me." Another pause, a clearing of his throat. "I've kept it
inside for too long…"

Elizabeth sat very still, waited. She didn't like the way he'd
begun toying with the fringe on the edge of the pillow, like he'd
grown agitated and couldn't settle down. Everett Broderick was
not a man to fidget. "Uncle Everett? What's wrong?"

"I've been waiting for this day for a long time, two years actually." He smoothed the fringe on the pillow, flattened his hand over it. "I told myself if I went before your parents, then that was a sign the truth should stay buried. But, if I survived them, that meant it needed to be told." He slid his gaze to hers. "To you."

"Truth?" She sucked in tiny breaths of air, tried to remain calm. She didn't like secrets or surprises, had always preferred straight-up answers that didn't attempt to hide facts or disappointments. "Just tell me, please?" There'd been so much secrecy between her parents, as though they shared a whole other world they never intended to share with her.

Uncle Everett set the pillow aside, blew out a long breath. "Your father and I did some bad things, Elizabeth. We stole money from the ad company where we worked. I did the books so it wasn't hard to move a few hundred from one column of the ledger to the other. Who would know? The owner was an old man who cared more about playing golf and drinking martinis than the bottom line. As long as he could do both, he wouldn't ask questions. We got bolder and started taking more money. Phillip manipulated the sales sheets and I massaged the numbers."

"You embezzled from your old company?" She'd thought they'd earned the money they used to start their real estate business through hard work, talent, and long hours. But to learn they'd stolen it was unfathomable, and yet, he'd just admitted it.

Uncle Everett's head dipped. "We stole, pure and simple."

"But why?" What could have turned them so desperate to make them steal?

His expression softened and he almost smiled. "Ah, Elizabeth, we did it to please your mother, who as you know, could never be pleased for long, no matter the quality of the diamond or the grade of the silk."

"You did this for Mother?"

He nodded his salt-and-pepper head. "Nobody could ever say no to her, and she knew it."

"Did she ask you to steal?"

The almost smile faded. "Your mother never had to ask. You know that."

Yes, she did. Sandra Hayes had been a beautiful woman with a smile and a way about her that made it hard to say no. She'd lived a life of wealth and privilege, with the finest of everything: clothing, jewelry, cars, trips. But it was never quite enough, not for long. The thirst for more ruled her world and when the boredom set in, her eager subjects rushed to bring more treasures home to the kingdom. How well Elizabeth knew about trying to please a mother who would never be pleased.

"I just wish we'd have left it at that. Why couldn't we have been happy with a little extra cash that nobody missed? Why did we have to go after a town that couldn't afford to lose what they had, and a man who wouldn't survive the disgrace? We're responsible for destroying families...ruining lives." His voice cracked. "I've regretted my part in it from the day it happened two years ago."

"What are you talking about? Whose lives did you destroy?"

He blinked back tears. "We destroyed good people whose worst crime was trusting the wrong person. We made promises we never intended to keep." He sighed, dragged a hand over his face. "Your father showed up in their small town under the alias of Gordon T. Haywood, promising what those people needed more than anything: hope. The most respected person in town was a man named Jonathan Donovan. Hard worker, honest, good family man." Pause. "Had a wife and a couple grown kids, owned an old factory building that needed a new tenant. Your dad told him he was in the business of assisting small start-up manufacturing companies. He said he could help him create a new business, renovate the place, and bring back jobs. Can you imagine what that sounded like to people who'd known their share of hardships? Everybody was excited, thinking about the money they'd make, and Jonathan Donovan was going to run the place and give jobs to thirty people…"

"But?"

"Of course, there was a catch." He pulled a handkerchief from his back pocket, swiped his eyes. "There's always a catch when your father's involved."

She didn't miss the remorse in his voice, mixed with a tinge of bitterness. "What did he do?"

"He convinced Donovan to take a loan against the property and give the proceeds to him, said part was to buy equipment and the other part was to pay the crew to work on the building. Making a deal like that would ensure that Donovan ran the company; that's what Phillip told him. Poor guy never saw it coming. He talked other people into investing in the business, used your dad's story to sell them on the idea of a locally owned factory. When people applied for a job, they got a form to fill in their investment amount. Forked over the money on the spot and even got a nice sticker that read *Thank you for believing*. A few hundred here, a thousand there, and the big chunks of money from Jonathan Donovan and his siblings from the mortgage on the building. Your father left town on a Friday with the promise that renovations would start that Monday." Uncle Everett looked away, his voice dipped. "Monday came and went with no renovations, same thing for Tuesday. I heard when Wednesday rolled around and Gordon T. Haywood didn't show, the town wanted to come after Donovan and take their anger out on his hide. It crushed him when he realized he'd been duped. He never recovered; turned to drink, died a broken man about a year ago."

Elizabeth tried to comprehend what she'd just heard. "How could you let that happen to innocent people?"

He shook his head. "I'll never forgive myself, not as long as I live."

"But why them?"

"I don't know. Your father picked the town; he was very insistent about it." He paused, squinted as though recalling the conversation. "Your mother found out about it and begged him to choose another location. That was the only time she got involved in business, legal or otherwise. It was also the only time I ever heard them argue. Your father wouldn't change his mind, and I knew better than to ask why he was so adamant about that particular town." He leveled his brown gaze on her. "Never did figure it out."

"Why did you tell me this? Why couldn't you have buried it with my parents?"

"Because we did that town wrong, Elizabeth, and I can't go to my grave without trying to right those wrongs." A tear trickled down his thin face, followed by a second. "I couldn't do it while your parents were alive, but now I can." He paused, his voice thick with emotion. "And you can help me."

2

Elizabeth had always known there were gaps in her family life, secrets that created chasms of uncertainty and loneliness where her parents were the united force, and she, the stranger. Uncle Everett's sickening revelation three weeks ago had filled in so many gaps. But there were many more that wouldn't be answered or even understood until she visited the small town that had suffered at the hand of her father's treachery. Uncle Everett had to share in the blame as well. But what of her mother's strange behavior? Why would a woman who'd never concerned herself with business or business dealings challenge her husband? Common sense said if there was a challenge, it should be about the scam and *not* the location for the scam.

She didn't want to be a part of any of this, and she certainly didn't want to pretend she knew nothing about how the town had been cheated and a man ruined. Still, if Uncle Everett believed she could right the wrong he and her father had done, then didn't the Donovan family deserve that?

Yes. Absolutely.

There were three files, plumped out and stuffed with details about Reunion Gap and its residents. Elizabeth had spent hours studying the contents, memorizing names, occupations, and dates as though preparing for a test. There were photographs, too, some as recent as a year ago. Uncle Everett's conscience had not permitted him to forget what he'd done and he'd secured an investigator to follow the town. But he'd been smart about it because no stranger would go unnoticed in a small town. That's why the investigator hired one of Reunion Gap's own, on the condition of anonymity, to submit updated information as well as photographs.

Lester is a very thorough investigator. All of the details, at least as many as a person can know without living in a place, are included.

So, you followed these people for two years?

Yes and no. Your parents never knew about it. I paid medical bills, tuitions, real estate taxes...it was all very delicate, but between the two of us, Lester and I made a good team. The only family we couldn't assist was the one who needed it most.

The Donovans?

Indeed. The father refused to listen to his own family, preferring instead to lose his days in drink. The son has made it his personal mission to help everyone in need, whether or not his father's poor judgment caused them harm. If he doesn't lighten his load soon, he'll end up no better than his father, probably worse.

How sad.

It's very sad, but you can change that.

How?

You're going to visit Reunion Gap, tell people you've been hired to create drawings for some eccentric who's obsessed with your work and the Alleghenies. I'll be that man so it won't be a complete lie. Once you're there, you'll tell them you're thinking of staying the summer. That should give you enough time.

Time?

Indeed. Time to gain the younger Donovan's trust. He's the key to this whole deal. His name is Rogan. If you can do that, we

*can make this right, Elizabeth. We can give these people back
their hope.*

~

OLIVER ROLLED out of bed at 6:00 a.m. every morning, long
before his partner opened an eye. He'd had a lot of partners, but
this one was the best. She didn't sulk when he went out alone,
rarely whined, and except for the occasional back talk, was the
perfect companion. Not a fussy eater either. There was the rare
spurt of jealousy, but only when her competition came sniffing
around.

Yup, Maybelline was the ideal companion.

But then, most of his four-legged companions had always run
circles around the two-legged ones in terms of personality,
generosity, and compassion.

Oliver padded to the bathroom, showered, and tossed on a T-
shirt and jeans. Hope was stopping by to help him organize the
CD mess he'd inherited from his sister. For a nine-year-old, Hope
Merrick had a sense of organization that was better than most
adults. Maybe it was because she wasn't like other nine-year-olds.
She was shy—okay, a lot more than just shy—and preferred to
spend time alone, practicing her keyboard, reading, living in her
own dream world. Last month, she'd started composing a new
song and finished the latest Harry Potter book. So, the kid didn't
get invited to birthday parties and wasn't interested in the newest
fad. That didn't make her pitiful. She had a lot going for her and
if that overprotective mother of hers would let the kid find joy on
her own terms instead of trying to map out paths to successful
"adjustment," maybe Hope would blossom. Like a calla lily or a
hibiscus. But no. Jennifer Merrick wanted her daughter in a
cookie-cutter lifestyle where the woman could observe and tweak
as necessary to achieve the desired resulted. What a crock! He

pushed Jennifer Merrick and her constrictive expectations from his brain, turned on the coffee pot, filled Maybelline's bowl, and made his way to the back door.

The pale grayness of early morning spread across trees and dew-covered lawns in a majestic sweep of serenity. Birds flitted from branch to branch, their chirps filling the air, their small bodies graceful. He breathed in the crisp scent of morning and coffee, comforted by both. Of all the places he'd been, he'd never enjoyed the peace and calm of a place like Reunion Gap. Sure, there'd been heartache and sadness here, and the occasional double-dealing from less-than-trustworthy residents like the Alexanders. But for the most part, the town had stuck together until an outsider strolled in with a handshake and a promise and cheated them out of what mattered most: their hope.

If only his brother had been able to forgive himself and find a patch of happiness in the charred mess Gordon T. Haywood left behind. But Jonathan wasn't built for screw-ups that hurt others and left them bitter and angry. That had always been Oliver's arena and he'd done a damn good job of the screw-up part until a few years ago. He wished he'd been in town when Haywood was doing his dirty work and convincing his brother that the manufacturing company was about to be resurrected.

He dragged a hand through his wet ponytail, made his way back to the kitchen and poured a cup of black coffee. There was something to be said for having your place of work a few footsteps away from where you lived. When he bought the old house several years ago, he hadn't moved back to Reunion Gap yet, but he figured its location on the edge of Main Street might serve as a place of business as well as a home. At the time, he'd had no idea what that business might be. It wasn't like there'd be a huge demand for an aging rock-n'-roller with a talent at the keyboard and the ability to recognize a tune in three chords.

What did a person do with those skills other than impress

people at parties and in casual conversation? That had been the ongoing dilemma and yet, his brother hadn't thought it an issue at all. In fact, he'd called it a gift and an opportunity to make a business out of what Oliver loved. Oliver's Jukebox had been Jonathan's idea, along with a way to set up the place, decorate it, play vinyls on certain days, even offer keyboard lessons. This from a man who worked in a factory and claimed he wouldn't know creativity if it landed in his lap. Jonathan classified the idea of the music shop as "giving assistance" and brushed off Oliver's attempts to tell him otherwise. Had there ever been a more modest, compassionate, generous man? No, indeed there had not been. But his brother had been too modest, too compassionate, too generous. The perfect prey for a man like Gordon T. Haywood.

By the time Hope showed up at 8:00 a.m., Oliver had taken Maybelline for her morning walk, read the newspaper, eaten a bowl of oatmeal with blueberries and walnuts, and watered the petunias. When the front door of the shop opened, the string of bells tinkled. Maybelline barked and bounded off her bed toward the door, compact body wiggling, nails tapping the tile floor. He'd had to Maybelline-proof the shop against that rambunctious French bulldog's body several times, but even then she usually managed to knock over an item or two.

"Oliver?"

He pushed his reading glasses on top of his head, grinned. "If it isn't my little helper and Maybelline's best buddy." Oliver stood, made his way toward the young girl with the red hair and big dimples. "How long can you stay?"

She checked her pink wristwatch and said, "Mom said I have until 11:45."

"Oh, she's giving you an extra half hour this time, huh?"

Her eyes sparkled and her red curls bobbed up and down.

"Unless you have women come in. Then Mom says I have to call her right away."

For the love of…. Would that woman never stop her righteous comments? It's not like she'd been a saint, because if she had been, there'd be a father in the picture. Maybe he'd even live in the same house. But no, that wasn't the case, so The Righteous One wasn't exactly "righteous." But she sure was judgmental.

"So, do you have any woman coming because I don't want to leave?"

He couldn't resist asking. "Why would you have to leave?" Since the first time he saw Jennifer Merrick at the Cherry Top Diner, he knew she'd cause him a world of headaches. Maybe it was those sad eyes or the guarded expression she wore that said she'd been hurt and wasn't about to get hurt again. Or maybe it was because she reminded him too damn much of the woman who'd crushed his heart a lifetime ago.

Hope peered up at him. "Mom says you might want to entertain them." She scrunched up her small nose. "How would you entertain them? Does she mean play the keyboard and stuff?"

He hid a smile and ruffled the curls on top of her head. Jennifer sure did have a low opinion of him. Entertain women? What did she think he was going to do—bring them in the back room and engage in unseemly acts with them while Hope sat behind the counter, thumbing through comic books? The girl's next words confirmed that her mother's opinion was even worse than he suspected. "Mom called you a hippie." She tilted her head to one side, studied him. "I don't think you're a hippie." Those brown eyes grew larger and her voice dipped to a whisper. "Are you?"

Oliver lowered his voice to match hers. "No, I'm not a hippie."

She nodded, her expression serious. "I knew that."

"Tell you what. Next time your mom talks about me, tell her

to give me a call. I'll make sure you have my cell number before you leave."

"Okay." Another nod. "And I'll make sure you have Mom's number, too. Just in case you want to ask her anything." She held his gaze. "Like, does she want to go on a date with you."

Where had that come from? Oliver slugged down the rest of his coffee so he'd have time to come up with a response. But three more cups wouldn't give him enough time to respond to that one. *A date with Jennifer Merrick?* Hardly. The woman would skewer him if she knew he were half-interested in the possibility, and then she'd stick her nose up and tell him all the reasons he was unsuitable dating material—probably unsuitable, period. He was surprised she let Hope visit, but how could she argue with the deal they'd struck? Hope got keyboard lessons in exchange for helping him organize the music shop. The girl loved her music and Oliver loved an organized work place, but it was more than that, and he and Jennifer Merrick knew it. He was one of the few people Hope could relax around, probably because he accepted her for who she was, not who he thought she should be.

He liked Hope, liked the spunk in the kid, the curiosity and innocence and wonder. Why couldn't adults be more like that? Why did they all have to turn so serious, like they were sent here to save the world rather than provide small measures of comfort and kindness to each other while walking this earth? If they could all be more like Hope Merrick, Reunion Gap would be a better place; the world would be a better place. *Life in general would be a better place.*

But for now, all they had were wishes, past disappointments, and the beauty found in the innocence of a child.

And that would have to be enough.

"Oliver, can we go outside and water Jimi and Mick?"

She was talking about the herbs he'd named after his rock-n'-

roll heroes. "What about Rod? And Elton? And you better darn well not forget Keith because he already gets ignored enough."

∽

ELIZABETH DROVE into Reunion Gap on a sunny afternoon in late May. If she hadn't known the story behind the town, she'd have thought it was like any other small community, built on trust and a handshake where everyone knew everyone, knew their history, too. She'd been raised in an upscale suburb in Ohio, and the notion of anyone knowing too much about her was unsettling. Her parents hadn't had many friends and they'd never encouraged her to either. They'd told her their small family, including "Uncle" Everett, was cozy and just enough, but maybe the real reason they didn't want to expand their circle was a concern they couldn't keep their stories *or* their motives straight.

Hadn't Uncle Everett admitted he and her father had schemed to cheat businesses, two that she knew about? But what if there were more? And what if people from one of those companies traveled in the same circles as her family? That could cause a lot of problems if anyone started noticing discrepancies in the books.

There were so many questions and not enough answers, or at least not the right ones. Uncle Everett thought it best if she stayed with as much of the truth as possible when relaying information to the residents of Reunion Gap. *You won't have to recall your fabrications*, he'd said. *At least you'll be able to rely on some truths*. On that she agreed. How did a person walk into the town her father had damaged and inquire about the family of the man he'd destroyed? She'd memorized the names and faces in her uncle's folders along with details such as occupation, hobbies, even children's names. Sleep had eluded her these past few days as she imagined her first encounter with Rogan Donovan, the oldest son who'd returned to save the family.

It didn't sound as if he'd been successful, or at least not in great measure. From what the investigator's notes revealed, Rogan's father was dead, his brother's whereabouts were unknown, and his sister traveled the country and hadn't been home since Christmas. There was vague mention of Rose Donovan, the mother who possessed a weak emotional constitution and suffered a breakdown when her husband's ill-fated decisions threw them into financial ruin.

Rogan Donovan was the key to making Uncle Everett's plan work. She'd studied his picture, committed to memory the close-cut, chestnut hair, the brackets around the mouth that might or might not become dimples when and if the man smiled. And then there was the intensity in those blue eyes that pulled her in, made her catch her breath. Could she convince him to let her invest in the company? How would she do that without divulging her real identity or her true purpose?

Elizabeth gripped the steering wheel, sucked in a deep breath and turned onto Main Street. She spotted a diner, a bank, a hair salon, and the post office. There was also a clothing boutique, a jewelry store, and a music shop. There were more stores, but within thirty seconds, she'd passed all of them. According to Uncle Everett, there were two major families in Reunion Gap: the Donovans and the Alexanders. They didn't care for one another, something about an Alexander stealing a Donovan's wife back in the day. Or was it the other way around? It was all speculation, and the investigator's source said it happened so long ago that many considered it a tall tale stuffed with more fib than fact. Whatever the reason, the animosity still existed.

She spotted the Peace & Harmony Inn, a log cabin bed-and-breakfast a quarter of a mile outside of town on a quiet street filled with maple trees and clusters of impatiens, petunias, and geraniums. Elizabeth pulled the SUV into the driveway of the inn. According to its website, Peace & Harmony was the only overnight accommodation in town and boasted home-cooked meals, afternoon tea, and a honeymoon suite with a queen-size bed strewn with rose petals. Rose petals?

Wouldn't the petals make a mess? How did the innkeeper prevent them from withering? While some might consider the petals romantic and heart-warming, Elizabeth would much prefer a bouquet of roses in a vase. On a night stand. Better yet, why not a single rose in a bud vase? Didn't that exemplify the beauty of one? If it were up to her, she'd ditch the rose idea and settle on a bouquet of tulips or forget-me-nots...or maybe a cluster of daisies. But then, nobody had asked her and because she didn't possess a romantic bone in her overly sensible body, nobody ever would.

She grabbed her suitcase and art bag, hopped out of the SUV, and headed toward the front steps of the log cabin inn. A second of dread overtook her as she walked up the stamped sidewalk. Would she be able to pretend she knew nothing of the town or the misfortune that had befallen these people, especially Jonathan Donovan? Could she act as though she didn't know about the long-standing feud between the Donovans and the Alexanders, a feud that might never end? And when she met Rogan Donovan, would she be able to smile and tell him the natural beauty inherent in the Allegheny Mountains drew her here?

How on earth was she going to do it?

The front door opened, shutting down her questions. "Elizabeth Hastings? I've been expecting you."

The use of the fake name caught her off guard, but she recovered, worked up a smile for the woman who stood on the other side of the threshold. Late thirties, wavy brown hair, blue eyes. Approachable. "Yes, I'm Elizabeth." She'd have to do a better job with her delivery because Uncle Everett said no one would believe her stories if she didn't make them sound credible—as in, she had to believe them herself. He'd insisted on the semi-fake name, telling her a person couldn't be too careful.

"I'm Jennifer. Welcome to the Peace & Harmony Inn." The woman took the suitcase and carried it into the foyer, her dangle earrings swaying with the motion. She was three or four inches taller than Elizabeth, with a light smattering of freckles across her nose. "It's usually pretty quiet around here, not a lot of commotion with children running around." She paused, her voice slipping a few notches. "I have a daughter." Another pause. "She's not the rambunctious type. In fact, Hope is nine going on thirty-nine. She's very shy so you might not see her, and if you do, she might not speak."

"Thanks for letting me know." Elizabeth had no experience with children, no nieces or nephews. Children made her nervous; she had no idea how to relate to them, what to say or not say. But a shy child who acted like an adult? *That* she could certainly relate to since it pretty much described *her* childhood.

"Come on in the kitchen and I'll fix you a glass of iced tea or coffee, whichever you prefer. I just baked a batch of chocolate chip cookies."

Small-town hospitality served with a plate of cookies and a beverage. Could it get any better than that? Elizabeth's mother hadn't baked, preferring to make a list for the cook. Oh, but the house had smelled so good when Dottie pulled sugar cookies or brownies from the oven. Sadly, Elizabeth had no culinary skills, but how could she when she hadn't been permitted to experiment in the kitchen and helping the staff was not encouraged? There were so many areas of her life that were lacking. If her parents had only taken the time to guide her, her world could have been so different. She might have found a way to belong.

But they hadn't taken the time.

And she'd suffered because of it.

Jennifer led Elizabeth down a hall covered in knotty pine

paneling, opened the kitchen door, and motioned for her to sit at the oak kitchen table. "Tea, brewed or iced? Coffee? Water?"

"Iced tea, please."

Jennifer glanced up from the cooling rack of chocolate chip cookies, held her gaze. "Not a lot of people know about the Peace & Harmony Inn." She swept a hand in the air. "It's more of a romantic getaway place." When she realized what she'd said, she stumbled to recover. "Not that it's only for couples or that you aren't part of a couple…that's not what I meant." She shook her head, a faint pink creeping from her cheeks to her chin, slipping down her neck. "Goodness, forgive me. I'm never this careless with my words."

"I'm not offended." Elizabeth shrugged. "Being solo is a lot better than being with the wrong person."

Jennifer Merrick's blue eyes turned bright, shimmered. "Yes. That is absolutely true."

There was heartache in those words. Had this woman known what it was like to be with the wrong person? Had Hope's father *been* that person? Elizabeth had taken great pains to not get over-involved in her relationships, so much so that her last significant other had called her cold and unfeeling. That wasn't true. She did feel; she felt a lot. The problem was feeling too much, an issue she'd had since she was a child. What had such emotion ever brought her but heartache and disillusionment where no matter how hard she tried she was still the outsider? She'd experienced it with her parents, her first boyfriend whose parents were close friends with hers, and the few in between—all carbon copies of selections her parents would make for her: wealthy, driven, more interested in the trappings than the person.

How did someone change habits and beliefs that had been ingrained since childhood?

Would she forever be destined to make poor choices when it came to choosing a partner?

Or was she simply meant to be alone?

"So, what brings you to Reunion Gap?"

She stifled her thoughts, turned back to the innkeeper. "I'm an artist. I travel to different parts of the country and draw nature as I see it. Flowers, trees, birds, streams, whatever captures my attention and my imagination."

"Oh." Jennifer handed her a glass of iced tea and gestured toward the plate of cookies.

The tepid response meant the woman had no idea what she was talking about, or how traveling around, drawing nature, could be classified as a job. Elizabeth heard it all the time. People usually got stuck on the drawing-nature-as-a-job part because it didn't fit into a typical category as a reliable source of income. "Even though I live one state over, I've never taken the time to visit Pennsylvania." She'd wanted to spend a summer in this area, drawing and creating what nature chose to reveal, but her parents convinced her such a venture would be the grandest waste of time.

Why would you want to go there?

Wouldn't you rather travel to Virginia or North Carolina? Or what about Kentucky? Texas? Certainly, you'll want to go back to California, won't you?

Elizabeth had wanted to please them so much that she shut down her dreams of visiting the rugged beauty nestled at the foothills of the Allegheny Mountains. Now she had a chance to do just that, and the fact that she was on a mission to help the family her father had cheated was bittersweet.

"You should see this area in the fall." The emotion in Jennifer's voice spilled over her. "There's nothing quite like it. People come from all over to see the leaves. And winter? That is a *must* experience. The fresh-fallen snow sparkles like a blanket of jewels." She slid Elizabeth a smile. "How long did you say you were staying? A season or two?"

Elizabeth laughed, picked up a cookie. "Not quite that long." And just like that she dropped in the quasi-truth. "I've been hired by an eccentric to draw the flora of this region. Seems he's obsessed with my work and the Alleghenies." She shrugged, glad Uncle Everett had given her a plausible story that was at least part true. "What about you? Were you born here?" Of course, she already knew the answer to that. Jennifer Merrick had moved to Reunion Gap ten years ago and had a nine-year-old daughter named Hope who suffered from extreme shyness.

"I moved here when I was pregnant with Hope." Her words were cautious, her expression guarded. "I've been here almost ten years."

"Does the town still consider you an outsider?"

The innkeeper looked away, toyed with a spoon. "Unless you were born here, you'll always be considered an outsider. But, we've learned to cohabitate, and that's more than I can say for some families."

There was a message in those words. Jennifer and her family hadn't gotten along. Elizabeth knew what it felt like to be on the outside of a family, trying to win approval, or at least, acceptance. Is that what had happened to Jennifer? Before Elizabeth left town, she'd like to find out. "I've been to a lot of small towns and the people have always been gracious and welcoming. I think that's one of the reasons I gravitate toward small towns." This was true, no embellishment necessary.

Jennifer shot her a gaze that said she was way off base if she thought Reunion Gap was one of those towns. Her next words confirmed the meaning behind the look. "This town doesn't welcome strangers, certainly not ones who come poking around, asking questions. Yes, we have tourists who enjoy the sights, but they don't stay and when they're here, they just want the experience of driving five miles for chicken wings and ice cream, making it through downtown in less than twenty-five seconds.

Hiking the trails, breathing the fresh air, swimming in our lake. They want a story to pack up and carry home with them." She paused, lifted a shoulder. "Whether it's the truth or not."

"Meaning?"

"They don't know any more about this town when they leave than they do on the day they arrive. They'll tell tales about this person or that, but it's not the real story because this community will never open up to a stranger and let them see what really happens here."

"And why is that?"

"Because it's not their business." Her blue eyes narrowed, and the thinness in her voice spread across the table, gripped Elizabeth. "They're strangers here and that's how they'll leave."

If this were true, what would the town say when she made it known she planned to stay for the summer? And how on earth would she convince this Donovan man to let her invest in his company? Why hadn't Uncle Everett told her the challenge she'd face would be next to impossible to achieve? She knew about shutting people out, had done it all her life. Still, there must be a way... "You found a home here. How did you do it?"

The woman's lips pulled into a slow, sad smile. "The town wasn't always like this. It used to be warm and welcoming, like most other small towns." The smile drooped, pulled into a frown. "And then one man showed up in Reunion Gap and everything changed."

Gordon T. Haywood. Her father. Elizabeth didn't need confirmation to know that's who Jennifer meant. But because she had a story to create, she asked the obvious. "What man?"

Jennifer didn't hesitate. "The man who destroyed our town and ruined one of the most respected men in our community. If you have questions, you're going to have to go through Rogan Donovan to get them." She tilted her head, studied Elizabeth. "You'll know him when you see him."

3

Camille Alexander swooped into Elizabeth's life in a flash of jewels and high-end fashion. The petite woman with the fiery red hair and calculating stare found Elizabeth the next afternoon at the Cherry Top Diner.

"You must be Elizabeth Hastings." She didn't wait for confirmation or an invitation but slid into the booth across from Elizabeth and set her leather handbag on the seat beside her. A smile, an assessing look from those blue eyes, and then, "So, *you're* the new girl in town."

Elizabeth nodded, took in the woman's designer scarf draped around her neck, the silk blouse, the diamond studs. She'd grown up around people like this: moneyed, entitled, condescending. Her mother had been one of these people and, to a lesser extent, so had her father. And she'd hated it, hated that they believed a person's net worth defined their self-worth. She worked up a smile, forced the judgment from her voice. "News travels fast. And you are?"

A flash of perfect white teeth. "Camille Alexander."

"Nice to meet you." Elizabeth recognized the Alexander name as one of the feuding families in the files Uncle Everett had given her. But there'd been no mention of a woman named Camille. Who was she and how did she fit into the Alexander hierarchy?

The petite redhead lifted a small shoulder, rested her hands on the table to reveal a wedding band with five rows of the most brilliant diamonds Elizabeth had ever seen. Another diamond ring circled her right index finger, this one a single row, equally brilliant. "My brother told me you'd come to town, so of course, I had to check you out." She lifted her empty coffee cup, held it out to the waitress behind the counter. "I would have stopped at the inn yesterday, but I didn't get back from New York until late." Her laughter tinkled around her, suspended while the waitress poured her coffee and scurried away. "I don't know why that girl is afraid of me." She shook her head and *tsk-tsk*ed. "Timid as a church mouse." Camille Alexander darted another glance at the waitress, lips pinched, eyes narrowed. "But those are the ones you have to watch, aren't they?"

What did she mean by that? The waitress had been polite and curious when she brought Elizabeth a tuna on rye with a side salad. The curiosity had turned to enthusiasm when she learned Elizabeth was an artist. There'd been no evidence of a timid mouse, but then she wasn't as intimidating as Camille Alexander. "Would you like to join me for lunch?"

The woman studied the tuna on rye as though it were cat food. "No. Thank you. So, I hear you're an artist. Flowers and leaves, is it?" She sipped her coffee. "Do tell. How does one make a living drawing flowers and leaves?"

Camille Alexander's words mimicked the ones her mother had taken every opportunity to thrust at her. *You think you can draw for a living? There aren't more than a handful of artists who can earn a living through their work. A handful, Elizabeth, and you won't be one of them.* "I've been very fortunate." She snuffed out her mother's words, concentrated on the woman across from her. "There seems to be an interest in the work I do. In fact, I'm on a job right now."

She lifted a perfect brow. "Really?"

There was interest in that word, not feigned politeness or condescension. Elizabeth nodded, forked a piece of lettuce. "My client wants me to capture the natural beauty of this area. He's left the details up to me, which is both challenging and exciting." Uncle Everett *had* left the details up to her, and while that included drawings, her main objective was to find a way to get Rogan Donovan to trust her so she could carry out her true mission: repay his family for what hers took.

"Fascinating." Camille took another sip of coffee, bit into one of the chocolate-covered wafers the waitress had delivered.

Did Camille have a standing order here that negated interaction? There was something about the pretty young waitress this woman didn't like. Was it her youth? Or perhaps her beauty? Some women didn't want to be reminded that despite cosmetics, treatments, and surgeries, they were still going to get old. They refused to accept this fact, and it was this refusal that made them desperate, made them do desperate things—like demean a woman whose skin was still filled with elasticity and a natural glow that hadn't been the result of a cream or a procedure. Elizabeth had witnessed this with her mother, had felt the sting of her jealousy as she invested in high-end creams, beauty treatments, and surgeries in an effort to remain more beautiful than her daughter.

"I take it you didn't always make enough money selling drawings of flowers to buy a watch like that?" She pointed to the two-tone designer watch on Elizabeth's left wrist.

"It was a gift from my uncle." Another truth, but not the one Camille Alexander wanted to hear. She wanted to know more? Fine, she'd hear more. "If you're wondering how I got my start, I studied art in school, but I began drawing long before I went to college." More truths spilled. "When you're a shy child who doesn't know where she fits in, you find places to belong. For me, it was wandering outside, watching the bees and hummingbirds, waiting for a rose to open in full bloom. The sounds, the smells, even the quiet, were all magical and welcoming. They provided great comfort and became my home."

Camille's voice turned soft, curious. "When did you begin drawing?"

"I was eight or nine and my uncle found me studying a holly-hock bloom. He said if I could stand still that long, then maybe I could create what I felt. I didn't know what he was talking about at first, but once I started drawing, then I knew." She smiled, her half-eaten sandwich forgotten as she recalled the joy and sense of belonging she experienced whenever she began drawing her next subject. It wasn't about the money or the acknowledgment. It had never been about that. Passion guided her, led her down a path of wonder she'd never found anywhere else.

"It must be exhilarating to find a place where you truly have a sense of purpose."

Elizabeth eyed the woman for sarcasm but found none. "Thank you."

She nodded, her tone switching from wistfulness to in-charge. "You still haven't answered my question regarding how you got your start? Either you worked in a coffee shop or some other equally depressing job while you tried to make a go of it, or—" she leaned forward, her blue eyes sparkling "—you've got family money. Which is it?"

There was nothing shy about this woman who'd tossed aside politeness and burrowed to the heart of what she wanted to know. Elizabeth toyed with her fork, worked up a half smile. "Both."

Camille Alexander leaned back, nodded. "I figured as much. Bet you can make a mean espresso."

Elizabeth laughed. "I'm quite good at it. What about you? I've only been here a day and I've already heard the Alexander name mentioned several times. I take it your family's one of the main ones in Reunion Gap?" Of course, she knew they were but let the woman think she had no idea.

"Actually, there are two primary families in this town: the Alexanders and the Donovans." She eyed Elizabeth. "Can't stand each other, and I mean cat-fight-roll-in-the-mud can't stand." Her pink lips pulled into a slow smile. "I used to be a Donovan... before I married an Alexander."

"Oh." How had *that* bit of information not been in the file?

Camille Alexander laughed. "That's what the whole town said. It was quite a surprise when Carter and I wed." Her smile faded. "Back then, we were all about shocking our parents and proving everyone wrong." She cleared her throat, said in a low voice. "Not sure we achieved that goal." There was the slightest pause, followed by a shrug, and then, "Anyway, I've got someone I'd like you to meet. He's sweet when he wants to be, knock-down-drag-out gorgeous, and way too considerate." Those pink lips puckered. "But he's so damn serious, it's a shame. Has been since he rolled back into town to help his family two years ago. If somebody doesn't get him out of his funk, he'll be an old man with nothing to hold onto but a load of regrets."

Elizabeth clutched her fork, fidgeted in the booth. Camille Alexander wanted her to save somebody, a man no less? How could she do that when she couldn't even save herself? "I'm sorry, but I'm not good at rescuing people." Her attempt at laughter flopped between them. "You really don't want me involved."

The other woman offered a calculated smile. "But of course I do. I think the attention of a beautiful woman with class and a kind heart is exactly what my nephew needs. What? Why are you looking at me like I've gone mad? I owe my nephew; we all do for the way he's tried to rescue everyone, even the ones who don't want to be rescued. What happened wasn't his fault and yet he took it on his shoulders, gave up his home, his job…his fiancée. And nobody tried to stop him. They were all too deep in their own grief to realize what was happening until it was too late." She tapped a manicured pink nail against her chin, studied Elizabeth. "But now you're here and I see an opportunity for my nephew to live his life again, like a normal thirty-something man."

Was she referring to Rogan Donovan? Elizabeth had to stop her… "Mrs. Alexander—"

"It's Camille. I know what you're thinking but you haven't met my nephew. Just reserve comments until you do, okay? After you meet him, if you still think I'm crazy, then I won't bother you with my fancifulness again, but I don't think that will be the case." When Elizabeth continued to stare, Camille's smile spread. "I take that as a yes?"

"You should take it as a 'probably not.' I'm only trying to be polite."

"Of course you are. I can tell good breeding and you, Elizabeth Hastings, have very good breeding." She finished her coffee, set the cup aside. "Now, let's talk serious. My nephew's mother is practically homebound. Psychological issues and all that. Rarely goes out. We'll work through her. She's a true dear; too bad she's had such a difficult time." She grabbed a napkin, dabbed the corner of her eyes. "She lost my brother last year and would welcome someone like you to tell her stories to… You see, she lives in the past…" Camille reached across the table, patted Elizabeth's hand. "I can't wait for you to meet my nephew. You won't be disappointed; nobody's ever been disappointed in Rogan Donovan."

~

ELIZABETH HASTINGS.
  New girl in town.

Person of interest, as in, person to investigate.

Rogan eyed the woman over his iced tea as she answered his mother's questions about watercolor versus oil painting. Apparently, it made a difference which brush you used, something to do with chemical composition and viscosity. He wouldn't know. Was drawing flowers really a job? Could you make any money at it, or was it more of a hobby for those who already had money? His gaze slid to her handbag, leather, designer level, the simple but classy cut of her blouse, the shoes, more leather. Yup, he'd bet she had a closet full of high-end labels and a hefty bank account, too. He'd known a lot of women like that in his previous life, had even been engaged to one of them. But Deborah had bowed out when he'd headed back east to help his family. At the time, he hadn't planned on staying in Reunion Gap, had thought he'd assess the situation, assist with damage control, and fly back to California. His ex-fiancée hadn't liked that plan, said it was too cumbersome and infringed on their goals. *Infringed on their goals?* He still couldn't understand that one. How did a person abandon his parents when they needed him? He wouldn't do it and they'd argued, and then she'd returned the engagement ring and moved out as if their relationship were a pair of shoes that had grown too tight.

That was two years ago, but the memory still resurrected itself every now and again. Rogan would lay money down that Elizabeth Hastings was no different. Not that he cared because he wasn't looking for a woman *or* a relationship. He had a woman in the next town, a no-strings-casual-sex woman; why would he want more?

"Dear?" His mother touched his hand, leaned toward him. "I was just telling Elizabeth about your marinara sauce, how you grow your own tomatoes and herbs, and sometimes, you even help Oliver make pasta."

"Did you also tell her it's the only dish I know how to make, aside from scrambled eggs?" Why was his mother telling this woman about his culinary skills, or that he helped his uncle make pasta? Was she up to something, like trying to play matchmaker? Rogan rubbed his jaw, sighed. It was so damn difficult to be an adult with a parent in the house, especially one who insisted she knew the kind of girl that would make him happy.

"That's not true." Rose Donovan's laughter trickled over them like a mountain spring. "You're much too modest."

"I don't think so, Rose," this from Oliver. "I think Rogan stinks at everything he tries in the kitchen *but* his marina sauce and scrambled eggs. Ever see him try to poach an egg? Or fry one sunny-side up?" Oliver shook his head. "It's a disaster."

"Who needs to know how to cook when you have a line of volunteers?" Aunt Camille sashayed into the room, a drink in one hand, a tray of stuffed mushrooms in the other. She flashed him a wide smile and set the tray on the coffee table. When she set her mind to it, she was the best damn cook in town. People said she should have been a caterer but Camille Alexander shrugged off the compliment. Such an activity constituted a *job* and she wasn't interested in one of those. Too bad she let her social standing get in the way of what might actually make her happy.

"Rogan, no comment about volunteers in the kitchen?" She leaned close, gave him a peck on the cheek. "I know there's a long line, or there would be if you were open to the idea."

"Nope." He wished they were alone right now and not in the company of a stranger so he could tell his aunt to stop with the antics. He wasn't looking for a fix-up, and she could dance around the subject all she wanted with her *I have someone I know your mother will want to meet*, because they both knew it wasn't about his mother at all.

Camille wanted to play matchmaker.

Again.

If she'd just concentrate on her own issues with her two-timing husband, maybe she'd work up the nerve to dump his ass and file for divorce. But that probably wasn't going to happen, not when Camille Donovan Alexander had given up so much to join the Alexander clan and would have to admit the guy *and* the choice were bad decisions. If Rogan were a psychologist, he'd guess his aunt obsessed with the matchmaking for friends and family because her own love life was such a screwed-up mess. Still, people weren't pawns to be moved around on a relationship board so a middle-aged, less-than-happy woman with too much money and not enough causes to keep her busy could get through the day.

Rogan did not want to be her cause and he doubted Elizabeth Hastings did either.

"Do you cook, Elizabeth?"

Rogan sighed. The woman was not going to give this up.

Elizabeth blushed and stammered out an answer, "Not much and not well."

What was his aunt going to do with that one? He hid a smile, waited for Camille's comeback. She'd have one, no doubt about it, and it would be a good one, stuffed with just the right words and tone to make the listeners want to be a part of whatever she was peddling. Like hope, or possibility, or even a damnable second chance. Yup, mix them all together and see what shook out. But when the answer spilled out, it did not come from his aunt, but a most unlikely source—his mother.

"If you are ever in the mood to practice, you can borrow the kitchen anytime you want." Rose smiled at Elizabeth, her face lighting up. "And I'll be happy to give you a few lessons. There was a time I cooked everything from scratch, including the breads and desserts." Her voice filled with a sadness that spoke of loss and a past she wished she could recapture. She tilted her head to one side, darted a glance from Rogan to Elizabeth. "Would you like to come to dinner Wednesday? I'd offer Thursday, but that's his night with his—" she paused, tapped a finger to her chin "—what would you call it, dear?"

He'd call it his play night with Alyssa. Rogan cleared his throat, avoided his mother's gaze and mumbled, "It's just the night I grab a few drinks with friends and relax."

"Ah. Those friends sure smell nice." Her voice spilled over him like syrup. "And it's always that same fragrance. I notice it when I do your laundry."

"Mom." He eyed her, his voice stern. "This isn't the time."

His aunt's laughter spread through the room. "Indeed it is not, but maybe this will make Rogan consider his choice of *friends*." She threw him a pointed look that said, *I know about that woman you've been keeping company with, and so does your mother.*

"Goodness." Rose fell back against the needlepoint chair, put a hand to her mouth. "Did I say something I shouldn't have?" Her blue eyes grew wide, darted from Rogan to Elizabeth. "I'm sorry." She pinched the bridge of her nose, sniffed. "I'm sorry," she repeated.

"It's okay, Mom. No big deal." Rogan clasped her hand, worked up a smile. "Why don't you show Elizabeth your orchids? I'm sure she'd like to see them."

His mother perked up, her eyes bright. "That's a wonderful idea. Elizabeth, let's take a look at the orchids. They're exquisite if I do say so myself. Maybe you'd like to draw one when you come for supper? Will Wednesday work?"

Damn. Rogan glanced at Elizabeth who sat stone-faced still seconds before she murmured, "I'd love to come, Mrs. Donovan."

"Rose, dear. All of my friends call me Rose."

Then she stood, took Elizabeth's hand, and guided her toward the back of the house and the roomful of orchids, her prized possessions.

When they were out of earshot, Camille lowered her voice

and said, "Rogan, Elizabeth Hastings is a real jewel. Don't let her get away."

"Are you serious?" This from Oliver, who knew how to annoy his sister and make her accountable for her comments. "Why didn't you ask them to pick out china patterns? Come on, Camille, can't you go easy on them? You blindsided that poor girl and that was not fair. Rogan's a big boy and he can take care of himself, but foisting Rose on her? *We* still get weirded out by her behavior sometimes, and she's been like this for two years. You can't dump this crap on a stranger without warning." He cursed under his breath, stared at his sister. "It's not right and you should have known better."

Camille's glossy lips wobbled, pulled into a frown. "I'm sorry, Ollie. I just wanted to help."

"Well, you didn't." His tone softened. "You can't do stuff like this, Cammie. We talked about it, and you agreed."

Her head dipped. "I know." She sniffed, swiped at her eyes. "I just want to see Rogan happy after all he's done, and Elizabeth seems nice. Don't you think so?"

"She seems nice enough but you don't know a damn thing about her other than she's easy on the eyes and from the looks of the purse and clothes, comes from money." Oliver narrowed his gaze on his sister. "You didn't ferret her out because you think she has money, did you?"

"No, of course not." Her pale complexion turned the color of her red hair. "Well, not entirely. It was all part of the assessment. I didn't decide on the woman because I thought she had money, but I didn't *not* decide on her because of it either."

"I have no idea what you just said." Oliver sighed, scratched his stubbled jaw. "Rogan can pick his own women, Cammie. He's a big boy and he knows what he wants." Pause, another sigh. "And what he doesn't want. Like commitment and a decent relationship."

Camille's lips pulled into a smile. "So, you do agree that he's ruining his life with empty relationships that go nowhere." She landed her blue gaze on Rogan, her smile spreading. "But given time and the right woman, that could all change."

"He's got to be open to it, Cammie. You can't barge in and hand him a potential mate. It's got to be a natural progression." He nodded as if considering the process. "They've got to spend time together, get to know each other…"

"I like the sound of that. I saw the way they were looking at each other." It was her turn to sigh. "I remember those days: curious *and* interested."

"Excuse me, you do know I'm sitting right here, don't you?" Rogan had heard enough of their analysis regarding the status of his love life and his possible future with Elizabeth Hastings, a woman he'd met an hour ago.

Oliver grinned. "Of course we do, that's why we're doing it."

"Well, don't. And while we're on the subject of questionable behavior, do you really think it was a good idea to introduce her to Mom without a warning? We're used to Mom's behavior and most times we don't think twice about it, but what's that look like to a stranger?" *What did it look like?* Rogan didn't even want to think about it. If a person pieced together his mother's words, she'd sound like a woman in need of psychiatric help. Well, she had the help, and she had the medications. His mother had always been the fragile one, insulated and protected by her husband. But when he lost his reputation and his money to that cheat, Jonathan Donovan had become the fragile one, and Rose had slipped further into her own world. Now, Rogan was here to protect her, but he could only do so much because his mother still had her opinions and wasn't afraid to share them.

The most recent opinion was that her eldest son should find someone and settle down.

He loved his mother but that was *not* going to happen. No

more fiancée's and happily-ever-afters for him. He had his mother to care for and a furniture manufacturing company to start, and he didn't need or want the distraction and emotional upheaval a relationship entailed. If his siblings weren't traipsing around the continent right now, he'd ask them to come home for a visit and then see who their mother tried to match up with whom. Last he heard, Rose thought Charlotte would be perfect for Tate Alexander, as if that would ever happen. As for Luke, well, she said his soul mate was still out there. Somewhere. Right.

"Elizabeth does seem like a nice girl." His uncle followed Rogan to the kitchen, leaned against the counter. "I don't think she's the sort to judge. Seems compassionate and kind."

"And you determined this in one conversation?"

He shrugged. "I'm just stating the obvious."

"Uh-huh. The obvious."

"I've spent some time with her." Camille carried empty glasses and a beer bottle into the kitchen, set them on the counter. "I liked her. She's genuine, from what I could tell." She eyed Rogan, raised a brow. "You could do much worse, you know. And what exactly are you doing every Thursday night that covers you in a certain exotic fragrance? Hmm?"

He bet she knew all about other women's perfumes, had probably smelled enough of them on her husband's clothes over the years, but Rogan would never bring that up. One day his aunt might realize it wasn't okay or acceptable to be treated that way. And then, she'd fight back.

"Rogan, are you already involved with someone? Say so, because I won't have you two-timing Elizabeth."

"Two-timing? How can I be two-timing when I'm not even seeing her?" Sometimes his aunt made no sense.

"Ah." Those pink lips pulled into a knowing smile. "So, you are seeing someone. I thought so."

He tried to ignore the heat creeping up his neck. "I wouldn't exactly call it that."

"Leave him alone, Cammie. Can't you see Rogan isn't going to kiss and tell? Gotta respect him for that."

She tossed the beer bottle in the recyclable can, closed the lid with a thud. "If you say so. Fine then. I've made the introductions and that's all I can do. Elizabeth Hastings is a class act, and if you're not interested, that's your loss."

That was too easy. His aunt never gave in without a fight or a sarcastic comment.

"Maybe you really *are* destined to live your life alone." She met his gaze, held it. "I do hope not, because it doesn't have to be that way. People do get second chances."

If she believed that, wouldn't she dump her husband and get her own second chance? Her eyes glistened, like she was going to spill tears any second. He hated tears, didn't know what to do with them. "I appreciate your help." And then, because he couldn't stand the sad look on her face, he added, "I'll talk to Elizabeth, okay?" *Talk to her and what?* Hell if he knew, but the answer seemed to appease his aunt, because she burst into a big smile and hugged him.

She said her goodbyes a few minutes later, telling them she had a meeting with the decorator, and zoomed off in her new sports car. "That was interesting," Rogan said, washing a dish and setting it in the drain board.

"*Interesting* is a good word. Your aunt is a loose cannon. She's always been that way, and it's that recklessness that got her hitched to that jerk in the first place." Oliver glanced at the entry to the kitchen, lowered his voice, and said, "I heard he had a thing going with the new waitress at the Cherry Top Diner."

Rogan let out a disgusted sigh. "Are you kidding? What is she, all of twenty-two?"

His uncle shrugged. "I hear he likes them young." He opened

the fridge, peeked inside, and pulled out an apple. "Poor girls get all turned around by the M.D. after his name and the ten-dollar words flying out of his mouth."

"Yeah, I guess." Rogan grabbed a bottle of beer, twisted off the cap, and took a long pull. "We are one messed-up family, aren't we?"

Oliver looked up from his apple, shrugged. "All families are screwed up. Haven't you realized that yet? The question is to what degree? Take Harrison Alexander, head of the Alexander clan." He paused, studied his apple. "The man's got enough money to gold plate every toilet seat in his house if he wanted to, but that's not enough. He wants it all: the money, the power, the respect, and the control of this whole town." He pointed a finger at Rogan, frowned. "And that's never going to happen. The guy can sit on his piles of money but until *he* starts respecting people, including his own kids, he's not going to get that respect."

"Nope." Harrison Alexander was a mean-ass son of a bitch.

"And then there's us."

"Right, then there's us." There'd been a time when being a Donovan stood for strength, honor, and trustworthiness, but a stranger had destroyed that with his fancy words and empty promises. Rogan's father had not been able to recover from the disaster, and that had been his undoing. It had also marked the turning point in the family's sad story that left them disrespected and pitied.

"Screwed up doesn't have to mean screwed. We've all got issues, but that's not the point. The point is dealing with them and moving on." Oliver scratched his jaw, narrowed his gaze. "Like you, for example. You came home to help your folks, lost the girl because of it, and then you just gave up. Oh, you work hard with your spreadsheets and calculations, and you're helping people make better financial decisions. Hell, you're even working to restore your father's dream with the business. They're all honorable choices." His voice turned rough. "But what happened to the Rogan Donovan who had big dreams? Where'd they go? Where's the wife and kids? Where's the damn dog? You've buried them and it's a damn shame because you deserve it all." A soft laugh spilled from his lips. "Especially the dog."

Rogan stared at him, not sure if he should laugh or be pissed. Who was his uncle to talk about selling short on your dreams? "You talk a good game, but from where I'm sitting, you've short-changed yourself in those same areas."

Another laugh, this one louder. "You're full of crap. I'm doing exactly what I want."

"Good to hear. It's nice to see you've taken such an interest in Hope Merrick. How is Hope?" *How is her mother?* That's what Rogan really wanted to know. Oliver Donovan didn't talk about his women, and Jennifer Merrick was certainly *not* one of them, but it didn't take a fool to recognize the attraction between the two of them. Sure, they could deny it as long as they wanted, but sooner or later—

"Hope's fine. She's a whiz on the keyboard." Oliver developed a sudden interest in the apple core he held. "She's a good kid."

"Uh-huh." Rogan sipped his beer, studied his uncle. There was a definite I-don't-want-to-talk-about-this expression on his face.

Oliver shot him a look, his blue eyes dark. "What's that supposed to mean?"

"You know, I'll bet you and Hope's mother have a lot in common." Rogan paused, waited for his comment to settle in his uncle's brain before he continued, "If you'd ever stop denying it."

"I don't know what you're talking about. Jennifer Merrick and I aren't even in the same universe." Oliver tossed the apple core in the garbage, washed his hands. "Why are we talking about me? You're the one with a dinner date this Wednesday." He let out a laugh, the wrinkles at the corner of his eyes fanning out. "Do you want me to send over a bag of homemade pasta for you and Elizabeth? I've got some in the freezer. Pappardelle?" He winked, laughed again. "Yeah, this is going to be interesting."

When his uncle wanted to prove a point or let a person know he'd gone too far, nobody could match the man. Rogan got the message that he should have shut up about Jennifer Merrick when Oliver left—without Elizabeth Hastings.

"Your uncle said you might be able to drive me back to the inn? I'm sorry to ask, but he had some sort of minor emergency…"

Minor emergency? Right.

He took in the flushed face, the way she bit her bottom lip as if asking him for anything were the last thing she wanted to do. Okay, so he'd drive her to town. How horrible could that be? It wasn't like he had to engage in a long conversation; the ride was less than ten minutes. "Sure. No problem. If you're ready to go, we can head back now."

She nodded. "I'm really sorry to put you in this position. I don't mind calling a taxi or—"

"A taxi? We don't have transportation services in Reunion Gap." He stifled a grin. "It's fine. The inn is less than a ten-minute ride."

His mother clasped Elizabeth's hands and said, "I'll see you on Wednesday. Rogan and I look forward to it."

Could his mother be any more obvious? "Okay, Mom, I'm taking Elizabeth back now. I'll see you in a bit."

"Take your time." She smoothed her hands over the folds of her blue dress and nodded. "You're only young once." Her voice dipped, filled with sadness. "Enjoy it while you can and please, don't waste it."

"Right. Goodbye." He turned and flew out of the house, Elizabeth's heels click-clacking behind him. "Over here." Rogan pointed to his car, opened the passenger door for her, and made his way to the driver's side. "About my mother...." he said as he pulled out of the driveway.

"Please. You don't have to say anything." She stared straight ahead. "I understand."

"You do?" He glanced at her. "How can you when some days I don't understand it myself?"

"Your mother's hurting, isn't she?" A pause, a sucked-in breath, and then she turned to him. "I heard about what happened to your father. I'm so sorry."

Sorry? Yeah, the whole world was sorry, but nobody more than him. "Do you mean his actual death, or do you mean the incident that killed him but kept him breathing?"

"I...I...don't know what you mean."

The tone in her voice said she knew more than she wanted to admit. "You didn't hear about my father's fall from grace? How he invested in a bogus deal, took huge loans, and almost bankrupted himself and several families in town?" When she didn't respond, he figured what the hell, he might as well tell her because she'd hear about it soon enough. "Look, I'm used to the shock and disgust. It's okay, really. My dad was the most honest person I knew and unfortunately, the most trusting. Too bad there are so many people in this world looking to cheat innocent people. The guy who ripped off my father might as well have pulled a gun on him, because the way I look at it, he killed my father. And he left my mother to deal with the fallout, which, as you witnessed today, has been disastrous."

She cleared her throat, twice. "I'm so sorry."

"Thanks. And thanks for being so nice to my mom."

"She's a lovely woman."

"Yes, she is."

Lovely and broken-hearted. He thought about all the dreams his parents had, how they'd been the couple other people envied;

committed to each other, happy, in love. When Rogan moved to California, he had visions of his parents visiting him there, seeing the sights, meeting his friends, and eventually, his future wife.

And then it had all fallen apart.

Would it have been different if his parents hadn't loved each other so much? Would witnessing their destruction have been easier if they'd been just another couple married for a long time, and not the husband and wife who truly loved each other? There was no way to say, but Jonathan and Rose left scars on all three of their children: deep, painful scars that would stay with them long after the wound wasn't visible any longer. Rogan wouldn't let himself love, Luke couldn't trust, and Charlotte refused to love *or* trust.

Bad stuff. Dangerous. Insidious.

He pulled into the driveway of the Peace & Harmony Inn, shifted the car into Park.

"Rogan?"

He turned to face Elizabeth Hastings, wished she weren't so damn beautiful, so damn nice. "Yes?"

"I'm sorry your mother invited me to dinner on Wednesday." A faint pink crept up her neck, slid to her cheeks. "I'm sure it's the last thing you want to do, but I don't think I can get out of it. She seemed so happy, I didn't have the heart to tell her no."

He rubbed his jaw, pictured his mother's smiling face. "It's hard to say no to her. You don't mind coming?"

She shook her head. "If it makes her happy, then I'm happy to do it."

"Okay then. But there's something you should know. My mother's got it in her head that I need to find a wife." He dragged a hand over his face, laughed. "And she's decided that I'm not moving fast enough, so she's going to lend a hand."

"Oh. Well." She shifted in her seat like she wanted to bolt.

He didn't blame her. "Don't worry, I'm not looking for a wife, but I usually just play along."

"Usually?" She stared at him. "How often does this happen?"

"The matchmaking part?" He shook his head, sighed. "Whenever the opportunity arises, and if it doesn't, she creates the occasion. So, I'd like to apologize up front for the discomfort you're bound to feel when my mother starts her full-court press."

"Full-court press?"

"When she goes all out and really tries to match us up. Tonight was a warm-up."

4

Elizabeth had always been a loner and wasn't in the habit of sharing her opinions or her feelings with anybody else, especially new acquaintances. She'd guess Jennifer Merrick didn't have any issues sharing opinions or feelings because right now she was dumping a truckload on Elizabeth. Oh, she called it an observation but there was a lot of feeling stuffed in her comments, and that made Elizabeth wonder why the woman showed such emotion when she spoke of the Donovans.

She'd joined Jennifer in the kitchen this morning for coffee and cinnamon toast, begging off a fancy breakfast in the dining room. Cinnamon toast was a treat when her usual breakfast consisted of a yogurt and if she'd just been grocery shopping, a banana. Jennifer didn't sit while she ate, but mixed ingredients for a batch of double fudge brownies—her daughter's favorite.

"Don't let Camille Alexander cozy up to you because there's nothing soft or nice about that woman." Jennifer scowled, stirred the brownie mix faster, as though she might puree it. "Be careful."

"She was very nice to me, and very…direct."

Jennifer raised a brow. "That's a nice way of saying it. If she weren't such a pain in the butt, I'd actually feel sorry for her." She ran the spatula along the sides of the bowl, stirred one more time, and set it aside. "Nobody wants to be made a fool of, especially when you didn't see it coming." She let out a long sigh. "Though how she couldn't see it coming is hard to understand."

Elizabeth had no idea what the woman was talking about, and she didn't want to ask. Whatever truths were behind Jennifer's words were tied into Camille Alexander's pain and humiliation.

"Can you imagine your husband cheating on you with the waitress where you eat breakfast? Signing the hotel registry in the neighboring town as Mr. and Mrs. Carter Alexander? Guess the woman left a pair of earrings at the hotel and the manager shipped them home." She shook her dark head. "Talk about a mess."

Mess? More like a disaster. "I wish I didn't know this."

"Trust me, you haven't heard anything yet." She poured the brownies into a glass baking dish, smoothed the batter. "Poor Rose Donovan is so despondent over losing her husband that she's happier living in a make-believe world than a real one. And since her true love is gone, she's determined to help her son find his. It's sad and I really feel for Rogan. How humiliating." She eyed Elizabeth. "Better watch out or you'll be in the lineup." The blush must have given her away, because Jennifer's tone softened. "Ah, I see."

"He apologized and warned me, but it feels like we're both stuck in the middle, neither of us wanting to hurt his mother."

Jennifer nodded. "There could be worse torments than to be stuck with Rogan Donovan. What a hunk of a man; so darn sweet and way too appealing." She lifted the brownies, placed them in the oven and set the timer. "But don't worry, Rogan's not looking for a wife. In fact, he almost had one and she dumped him when he came home to help his parents."

"I'm so sorry."

"This town went through some bad times, but the Donovans went through the worst of it." She sank into the kitchen chair, rested her hands on the table. "Normally, I wouldn't say a word, but I don't want to see you get pulled into something and not know what's going on. Rose is a sweetheart, but she's not thinking clearly, and Rogan's a doll, but he's not looking for long-term parking. Then there's Camille, who's got her own definition of 'happily married.'"

"What about Oliver?"

Jennifer Merrick's face burst with an explosion of pink. She pursed her lips, sat up straight and said, "Oliver Donovan is an unfortunate alliance I tolerate because of my daughter."

"Unfortunate alliance?" What did *that* mean?

"Hope is extremely shy and doesn't have many friends. Scratch that." She cleared her throat and tried again. "She has no friends her age, and the person who makes her laugh and smile and act like a normal child is Oliver Donovan. He's teaching her to play the keyboard and he says she's a natural." She rubbed her temples, blinked hard. "How can I take that away from her just because I think the man is a womanizer in worn-out jeans and a ponytail?"

Elizabeth recalled the man's soft voice and kind eyes as he inquired about her drawings and asked how she liked Reunion Gap. He'd never probed or persisted when she'd hesitated with her answers. What touched her most was the gentleness he displayed toward his sister-in-law and his patience with his sister. "I don't know about the man's personal habits, but I found him to be very compassionate. If he's able to help your daughter find happiness, then isn't that what's really important?"

"Of course." Jennifer Merrick clasped her hands to her chest, frowned. "It's just that I don't like the man, and I'm trying to decide if that's a reason to forbid Hope to see him, or if I'm letting personal prejudices cloud my judgment." Her eyes misted. "I don't know the answer to that and the worrying keeps me awake some nights."

"I've never had a child, but I've *been* that child." Elizabeth nodded when she spotted the shocked expression on Jennifer's face. "I know all about alone and being alone. Invisible to the world and not fitting in. If it hadn't been for my uncle, who wasn't even my uncle, I would have been completely lost."

A tear slipped down the woman's cheek, followed by another. "Your parents weren't able to help?"

Now that was a question. *No, they hadn't been able to help because they'd never tried.* The better question would be *why* hadn't they tried to help? Elizabeth shook her head, said in a soft voice, "No, they weren't able to help."

"I feel the same way. I'm not able to help Hope either. I don't understand her shyness or what's going on in her head. I was always an outgoing person; put me in a roomful of strangers, and I'll talk to all of them. Hope's not like that. I just want her to fit in, but the other children know she's different and they avoid her. Some call her a freak." She paused, heaved a sigh. "There are times I wonder if not having a father has caused or made the behavior worse."

There was such pain in that last statement, filled with equal amounts guilt and regret. What to say to that? *Sometimes it doesn't matter if there's a mother and a father sitting across the table. If they aren't engaged and interested in the child's life, she's bound to suffer.* "I think it's hard to tell the reason, but does it really matter? For me, the most important part was having someone who didn't treat me as an oddity. For Hope, maybe that someone is Oliver."

Jennifer groaned. "I know, but why does it have to be that man? Why can't it be anyone but him?"

～

THE SECOND TIME Elizabeth saw Rogan Donovan, he was dancing

with his mother to "The Blue Danube Waltz." Camille Alexander sought her out yesterday because as she said, *You have to know the sadness that's touched Rose Donovan's life so you can understand why she's the way she is.* And then Camille had proceeded to tell her about the beautiful Rose Donovan who had once taught dance, crocheted bridal handkerchiefs, and made wedding cakes. The woman possessed a talent and sophistication that would have garnered attention and accolades in any city, but she'd wanted no part of the noise or the commotion of too many people stuffed so close you couldn't catch a clean breath. She'd thrived on tranquility and the love of her family. Many called her a gifted woman who could sew an evening gown, needlepoint a chair, and wallpaper an entire house. Such creativity required special care, and who better to guard and nurture Rose than her husband? Jonathan and Rose lived a magical life, filled with love, commitment, devotion, and Saturday evening waltzes.

And then Gordon T. Haywood descended upon them and nothing was ever the same.

Some said Rose's fall from reality began the day her husband told her he'd been duped by a swindler and taken on debt he might never be able to repay. For frugal people like the Donovans, this was hard to imagine, and yet it was true. Worse, other families had followed Jonathan's recommendations and plunked their hard-earned money into the fake deal. Those families shunned the Donovans, refused to speak with Rose after church, stopped calling her for coffee, and cancelled their dance lessons. There were no more wedding cake orders. No bridal handkerchiefs. No more friends.

Nothing but silence and long days.

It would take a full year for those who'd lost money to take an interest in dancing again or extend an invitation for coffee, even though rumor had it many had been paid back by Harrison Alexander. But a year was a long time, too long for the Donovans.

Jonathan had taken up drinking to obliterate his failure, and Rose had begun living in a fantasy world where life was not cruel, harsh, or judgmental. Her husband was so lost in drink and self-recrimination that he didn't realize his wife's need for help, but her son did. Rogan had come home to Reunion Gap and vowed to help make things right. But while he worked as an accountant, offering substantial discounts to those who'd been affected by the bad deal in an effort to restore faith in his family, he could not get inside his mother's head and make her world the way it used to be. When she suffered a nervous breakdown a few months after Rogan's return, there were a few casual inquiries, even a note or two of sympathy, but nothing that spoke of concern for the friend she'd once been.

And now, two years after Gordon T. Haywood's visit, with the help of medication and therapy, Rose Donovan drifted in and out of her days, some good, some bad, some almost hopeful. She danced, she crocheted, she baked and grew flowers in her garden. Life was almost good.

"She always was some kind of dancer," Camille said in a soft voice, her gaze fixed on Rose and Rogan as they waltzed their way around a room that held nothing but a stereo and speakers resting on a small table.

Elizabeth watched the couple glide along the hardwood floor, mother smiling up at her son, yellow chiffon dress swirling about her legs, cream pumps matching her son's steps. Elegant. Graceful. She glanced at Rogan's aunt, cleared her throat. "I feel like we're interrupting something private."

"We are, dear, but doesn't Rose look radiant and utterly at peace?"

"Yes, she does."

"That's how I remember her, before this horrible mess happened. When the kids were young, Rose and Jonathan would push aside the furniture to make room for dancing. They taught all three of the kids the waltz, the jitterbug, even the tango." She let out a slow breath, whispered, "It was magical to watch them. You don't often see such engagement between parents and children, not like that. There was so much laughter, so much happiness." Her voice wobbled. "I wonder if the children ever think of those times or if they just remember what happened later…"

"I hope they remember," Elizabeth said. She pictured Rogan Donovan as a young boy gliding along the floor with his mother, his brother waiting his turn while their father taught their sister how to twirl. Where were those siblings now? Camille hadn't revealed much about them other than to say they didn't get home much and Rogan's brother had issues. Whatever that meant.

"We have the choice of blurring the lens of the past to recall the kindness or sharpening the view to see every flaw. The first helps a person accept the past, while the second tears fresh wounds with every viewing." Camille glanced at Elizabeth, her eyes filled with tears. "What's the point of recalling every flaw? Jonathan died because he refused to see anything but the stark hopelessness of a bad decision. That's the tragedy of a person who won't let himself make a mistake. He can't forgive himself when he does, and sooner or later, we all mess up."

"What about Rogan? Do you think he's like his father, unable to accept making a mistake?" It wasn't her business and yet she couldn't help but wonder.

"Rogan?" Laughter spilled from Camille's pink lips. "That poor boy is ten times worse than his father." Her expression softened and she lifted an arched brow. "Which is why he needs a woman to show him he's wrong. Not just any woman, because there are certainly enough spineless ones running around, but one with character and grit." Those lips pulled into a slow smile. "Someone like you."

"Me? No. *No*." What was the woman talking about? "I'm not here to find a man; I just want to enjoy the scenery, meet a few people, and draw my pictures." *And find a way to pay back what my father took.*

"Exactly." More laughter. "But you can't deny my nephew is a very tempting part of the *scenery*. Please, don't overthink it. If it's meant to be, it will happen, and if not, you can't fault an aunt for trying. Now, let's go join them, shall we?"

Elizabeth followed Camille, trying to snuff out the woman's words about her nephew finding the right woman, and worse, that *she* could be that woman.

No. Never. Absolutely not.

Rogan Donovan smiled down at his mother as they danced to "Moon River." Tall, lean, graceful in a white shirt and dark slacks, he was quite impressive, but add the gentle, protective look he gave his mother, and the man was pretty much irresistible. No wonder women were after him. When he spotted Elizabeth watching him, his expression turned guarded, his feet slowed. Seconds later, he leaned forward to whisper in his mother's ear.

Rose Donovan glanced over her son's shoulder, broke free of his grasp, and rushed toward Elizabeth. "Hello, dear!" She clasped her hands, squeezed. "It's so lovely to see you again. Thank you for coming."

"I wouldn't miss this." She smiled at the older woman. "Thank you for inviting me."

"Hello, Rose." Camille kissed her sister-in-law's cheek, waved a hand at her nephew. "Looking good, Rogan. I never tire of watching your moves." She laughed and winked when he blushed. "Dance moves, darling. Dance moves." She tilted her head to one side, tapped a finger against her chin. "Though no doubt you've got a few other moves that have proved quite successful for you in the past."

He coughed, cleared his throat, and turned to Elizabeth. "Hello. Nice to see you again."

Before she could respond, his mother cut in. "Did you bring

your sketch pad? I was hoping we could spend time in the gardens." Her gaze darted from Elizabeth to her son. "And whatever else might be of interest. Rogan, will you fix us an iced tea? I'd like Elizabeth to try your special concoction. Would you mind?" She didn't wait for him to answer but barreled on. "We'll meet you outside. Camille, would you care for a glass of Rogan's specialty iced tea?"

"I was thinking I might like something a tad stronger to go with the iced tea." She winked and added, "I'll help you, Rogan. Lead the way."

"He is such a dear." Rose patted her son's cheek. "I couldn't ask for a better son."

Rogan Donovan's expression softened. "Go check your flowers and I'll be out in a few minutes."

Rose clasped Elizabeth's hand. "Come this way." She kicked off her pumps and stopped in front of the back door to slide into a pair of old sneakers. "Gardening is a messy job, but it yields beautiful results." She opened the door and motioned Elizabeth to follow. "This way, careful where you step." The back yard was scattered with flower beds bursting with color and a vegetable garden located toward the back of the property. "That's Rogan's garden. He doesn't see the practical side of growing something for the sheer beauty of it. But he's not an artist, not like you are." She sighed, ran a hand over a cluster of Russian sage. "Still, he's out here every spring amending the soil and rototilling the flower beds where I grow my annuals. And every Mother's Day, he buys me more perennials to plant. I have so many, but my son always finds me ones I don't have." Her voice dipped. "He takes good care of me."

Elizabeth ached for the woman who had once lived a full life with family, friends, and the man she loved, and was now diminished to moments of happiness and a past that was too painful to recall. How could her father have done this to these people? Had he ever stopped to consider the fallout of his actions? Or had he simply not cared because he was too busy trying to make her mother happy?

Was it always about making Sandra Hayes happy at the expense of everyone else, including their daughter? Her father might not have cared about Rose Donovan, but Elizabeth did, and she planned to do whatever was necessary to help her, no matter what that meant.

Rose's voice drifted to her, brought her back to the present with a gentle tug. "Sometimes I come out here at night and breathe in the fragrant air, gaze at the stars, and remember how life used to be when the children were little and Jonathan and I had such dreams. Those were the best times," she said in a soft voice. "The very best. We didn't realize it at the time, because we were so darn busy just trying to get through the day-to-day challenges of raising a family. We told ourselves that one day, life would settle down and we'd have everything we ever wanted; we'd take those trips we talked about, buy that camper, visit the kids wherever they ended up. Or maybe we'd just sit and do nothing. It didn't matter, as long as we could do it together." She clasped her hands to her chest, bowed her head. "We thought we had so much time…"

And then Jonathan met my father. "I'm so sorry, Mrs. Donovan."

"It's Rose, dear." She managed a smile, her eyes wet. "Thank you. I'm so glad you came back." Her gaze drifted over Elizabeth, her smile spreading. "You and I will be good friends, I can tell. Feel free to visit anytime you like, join me for an iced tea, sketch the gardens, let the scenery inspire you." She paused, her gaze shifting toward the back door and the man walking toward them, carrying a tray filled with drinks and cookies. "Yes," Rose Donovan murmured, "there's much to inspire, don't you think?"

Vague comments with double meanings continued through a

dinner of pappardelle with marinara sauce, salads, crusty Italian bread, and a bottle of Cabernet Sauvignon. Rose tiptoed around her comments, but Camille was bold-faced brazen about her innuendos.

Isn't it interesting that you both enjoy vineyards?

I find it refreshing Elizabeth prefers books to movies, don't you, Rogan?

Doesn't my nephew have the most compelling eyes? What do you think, Elizabeth?

And those dimples? Goodness, you both have them.

Rogan must take you to see the lake. Picture perfect. Pause. *And not a soul for miles.*

When the comments began, Elizabeth and Rogan avoided looking at each other, but after his mother and aunt's attempts to play matchmaker escalated, Elizabeth dragged her gaze to his and found him watching her. He leaned toward her and whispered, "This is ridiculous."

She nodded, whispered back, "Beyond ridiculous."

"Sorry."

"Not your fault." He met her gaze, his blue eyes dark. That was the kind of look a woman could get lost in…if she weren't careful.

"Rogan, why don't you and Elizabeth dance?" Rose clasped her hands together, her smile brilliant, hopeful, like a child awaiting the opening of a present. "I'm thinking 'Unchained Melody'? Oh, how your father and I loved to slow dance to that one."

"Mom, I've got a kitchen to clean up. You know I'm not the neat freak in the kitchen Oliver is." He offered a half smile. "How about you and Elizabeth listen to the music while Camille and I clean up?"

"Absolutely not." Camille pushed back her chair, stood, and began gathering the plates. "You two dance. Your mother can

61

relax and I'll clean up the kitchen." She let out a laugh and snatched up the silverware. "I haven't washed a dish in weeks, not since I hired the new maid. It will feel good to sink my hands in soapy water. Go ahead now. I'll fix coffee and dessert in a bit."

His mother stood and ushered Rogan and Elizabeth into the other room, turned to Elizabeth and said, "Thank you, dear. Thank you very much for coming into our lives."

If you only knew who I really am and why I'm here, I doubt you'd say that. Minutes later, Elizabeth stepped into Rogan Donovan's arms, and let the chords of the Righteous Brothers' "Unchained Melody" envelop her. Could there be a more romantic song than this one? Rogan's strong hand rested on the small of her back as he guided her, his other hand clasping hers. If Rose wanted to watch them dance and dream of her dead husband, it was a small gift to offer the woman considering the pain and damage Elizabeth's family had caused the Donovans. Soon, she'd ask Rogan about the manufacturing business that had been the source of his father's destruction. Once she saw it, she'd formulate a plan, and when the time was right, she'd offer to invest in it.

She'd use her father's money to do right by this family.

And she'd do it all without them ever finding out who she really was.

5

A man in a cowboy hat with a Texas twang doesn't walk into a small town like Reunion Gap and ask for a cup of coffee without getting noticed. Same thing had happened when he'd moseyed into Magdalena, but back then he'd been pretending to be someone other than who he was—an investigator on the hunt for answers. This time around, he wasn't hiding behind another persona, not that he was going to straight-out admit what he was doing in Reunion Gap, but at least the town would know who he was and what he did for a living. Investigators tended to make people edgy, and when a person got edgy, sometimes they revealed information they didn't even know they were revealing.

And that's what he was counting on to locate the daughter of a woman who'd seen more heartache than most in her life, including the disappearance of a daughter almost ten years ago. It was a voluntary disappearance precipitated by an argument involving a man of questionable integrity and intention, and ended with the daughter leaving town. Lester would not have gotten involved in the investigation if he didn't owe a debt to the town where the woman lived. In the past, he'd never questioned the motives of the person hiring him. He had a job to do and he was damn good at it. But Magdalena, New York, had been different, the people were different, and while he hadn't known or intended to harm them with his findings, he'd come close to destroying a few lives and almost broke up a marriage. He owed those people and he was going to make amends. How could he move to their town, marry one of their own, and *not* find a way to bring peace to one of the most respected people in the community? Truth was, he couldn't, and that's why he'd agreed to go on the hunt for Jennifer Pendergrass.

Of course, she could be going by a different name now, first *and* last. People did it all the time: disappeared into the fabric of another person's life or found a place where nobody asked questions or wanted answers. You could hide in plain sight. From what he knew about Reunion Gap, the town was filled with that sort, a good amount of mystery, secrets, and a feud between two families that would never be over.

Lester had never actually visited Reunion Gap but he'd been investigating it through a source for the past two years. The information he collected proved helpful and kept his client satisfied. But two months ago, his source mentioned one of the newer members of the town, a resident for the past ten years named Jennifer who ran a bed-and-breakfast. Jennifer Pendergrass's mother ran a bed-and-breakfast in Magdalena. What were the odds this was the long-lost daughter? So, her last name was Merrick? That meant next to nothing. There was only one way to find out if Jennifer Pendergrass and Jennifer Merrick were the same person, and that's exactly what he planned to do.

He opened the door to a small restaurant in the heart of town called the Cherry Top Diner and stepped inside. It was just after lunch and the tables and booths were mostly empty, though a few stragglers remained. The place had a cozy, rustic feel about it with soft lights dangling from the ceiling, putting an extra shine on the wooden tables and chairs. The booths were covered in burgundy vinyl with oak trim. If a person wanted to sit at the counter, he could take a seat on a swivel stool and get a bird's-eye view of what went on. Since marrying his waitress wife, he had a new appreciation for the ability to serve up food and carry on a conversation that sounded like you cared. There was no sign that read *Please wait to be seated* or *Please seat yourself* so Lester headed to the counter and waited for the young woman to finish with the coffee machine.

She slid a pot under the burner, pressed a few buttons, turned, and spotted him. "Can I help you?"

Timid thing, couldn't be more than twenty-two or -three, with big, brown eyes and a row of hoops traveling up her left ear. Lester removed his hat and nodded. "Yes, ma'am. I'm looking for a ham and Swiss on rye. Don't suppose you could fix me up with one?"

The young woman's pale lips worked themselves into a smile. "Yes, sir. We have the best sandwiches in town." She lowered her voice. "Everybody says so."

He lifted a brow. "Well then, if everybody says so, I think I'll have one."

She turned the prettiest shade of pink. "You won't be disappointed, and I'll bring you out a side of creamy potato salad to try. It's really good."

Lester followed her to the booth, slid his lanky frame into it. He'd guess the girl was small-town hospitable, which meant she might be a talker. That's how he'd gotten his wife to spill the beans about the comings and goings in Magdalena, but he didn't like to think back on a time when he'd fed her a line about why he'd come to her town. Medical supply salesman? Heck, he didn't know the difference between a suture and a bandage, and he was done pretending who he was to get information. "Nice place. I'm Lester. You the owner?"

The girl shook her dark head and her ponytail wagged back and forth like an English setter's tail. "No, sir. I just work here."

"Ah—" he glanced at her nametag "—Mindy. Nice name. Short for Melinda?"

Again, the ponytail wag. "Yes, sir. My father's name is Melvin and my mother's name is Linda. They couldn't decide, so they put their names together and came up with Melinda."

Lester grinned. "It suits you."

She blushed again, slid him a look. "I like your accent. Is that somewhere down south?"

"Texas."

"Oh." Her eyes lit up. "I've always wanted to visit Texas." Her voice dipped, turned softer than butter cream frosting. "I haven't been anywhere really. Just an occasional trip to Pittsburgh, and once to Niagara Falls. I want to travel." That voice grew softer. "Swim with the dolphins, see the pyramids. Eat pasta in Rome…"

"No reason you can't."

"That's what Carter—I mean, Dr. Alexander says." The pink in her cheeks turned cranberry. "He's been everywhere and he says if a person can dream it, there's no reason they can't do it."

"Well, it's a bit more complicated than thinking up a dream." Lester gentled his voice like he did when he was talking to one of his grandkids. "You got to have a plan, and you got to work the plan. Kind of like this place. You don't put items on the menu if you don't have ingredients or a way to fix them, right? You gotta have a stove, and a fridge, and a bunch of skillets and spatulas and such. All of that has to be in place or you can't advertise a ham and Swiss on rye or creamy potato salad." He cocked a brow and pointed to the showcase by the register. "And you don't want to advertise coconut cream pie if don't have any coconut."

"I see what you're saying." She tapped a pen against her chin, eyes narrowed. "Makes sense. Have a plan, work the plan." A small laugh escaped her lips. "I guess you could say make sure you have the ingredients so you can have success."

"There you go." Lester grinned. "I like that one, Mindy."

"I like it, too." She leaned toward him, lowered her voice. "I can't wait to share it. Thank you, Lester." She straightened and added, "Now let me see to that ham and Swiss on rye, toasted, with a side of creamy potato salad. Tea? Sweet tea? Coffee?"

"Coffee's fine."

She flashed him a smile, nodded. "I'll get right on it."

And then she disappeared, leaving Lester to wonder why she'd turned the color of a cranberry when she mentioned Dr. Carter Alexander and why she'd slipped up and referred to him by his first name.

The answer revealed itself as Lester walked down Main Street an hour later.

"Excuse me, sir?"

He turned to find a petite, fifty-something redhead staring back at him in an outfit he bet cost as much as a week at the Peace & Harmony Inn. "Ma'am?"

She eyed him from his Stetson to his cowboy boots, leaned close and said in a low voice, "Are you Lester Conroy?"

Camille Alexander. A man didn't forget the sound of culture and arrogance, especially when he lacked both. "Camille." How the devil had she learned he was in town? He'd planned to seek her out, but not until he'd formulated his own opinion of Jennifer Merrick. This was personal business and the fewer people involved, the better.

But it seemed like Camille was about to get herself involved.

The woman threw him a tight smile and motioned for him to follow her. "We need to talk."

When a woman said those words in a town he was investigating, it usually meant she had information for him. He followed her to a park bench, waited for her to say more.

"Let's have a quick chat. We've got five minutes, maybe seven before people get suspicious."

Lester waited for her to smooth her skirt and take a seat before he eased onto the bench beside her. "How've you been, Camille?" He'd spoken with her on the phone several times these past two years, shared emails, even a text or two. From the first conversation, he knew she was a firecracker who'd want to run the investigation if he let her. Camille Alexander was a natural at information gathering, and he'd told her as much. Big mistake. Give a person with an overblown ego a handful of praise, and they'll give you a bushel of grief. Still, he'd liked the woman for her ambition and her spunk. What he hadn't been too keen on, and what he'd tried to teach her, was formulating an opinion when not asked. As in, *don't butt in someone else's business*. He'd wanted details, *not* an analysis of what those details meant according to a wealthy socialite with too much time on her hands.

"Lester, what are you doing in Reunion Gap, and why didn't you tell me you were coming?"

"Hello to you, too, Camille. It sure is nice to finally match a face to a voice."

She let out a huff, her pink lips puckering like she'd tasted bad cheese. "Why are you here?"

He lifted a shoulder, crossed a booted leg over his thigh. "Just doing a little investigating."

Those blue eyes narrowed. "That was not the deal. I only agreed to help you because you said it would benefit my family." She paused, added. "Help right the wrong."

"Indeed I did, and I meant it. My turning up here has nothing to do with that job." He tapped his fingers on the leather of his boot. "This trip is…incidental, brought on by something that came to my attention through the information you provided."

She leaned toward him, whispered, "What kind of information? Are you investigating someone in Reunion Gap?"

Another shrug. "Could be."

"Who is it?" she hissed. "Is it my husband?"

Ah, it was always about that dang husband of hers. Lester didn't know why she didn't just dump the man, but his wife said sometimes it wasn't that easy, especially if love was involved. Maybe. Maybe not. Still, it wasn't for him to judge what people did or didn't do, or the reasons why. "No, Camille. It's not Dr. Alexander. Should I add him to the list? No problem to do a little digging."

"Absolutely not. That man's an open book and he doesn't care who reads the contents." She balled her small hands into fists, spat out, "Right now he's carrying on with that hussy from the diner. *Mindy*. Our children are older than she is."

So, Lester's hunch was right. Mindy, short for Melinda, named after Melvin and Linda, was tied up with Camille Alexander's husband. "I'm sorry to hear that."

She shook her head and red curls bounced about her neck. "I have no time for that man's nonsense right now. Who are you investigating?"

He shrugged. "I wouldn't call it investigating." He paused, rubbed his jaw. "It's more of a fact-gathering trip."

A sigh and an annoyed huff. "Who are you fact-gathering? It's got to be someone I know because I know *everyone* in this town. Is it one of my in-laws? Bet it's Harrison, isn't it?"

"Nope."

"Maybe I can provide information if you tell me who it is. Hmm. It's not a main player, is it? You said the information came through incidental gathering. That means someone who wasn't on the target list I provided."

Lester met her gaze, nodded. "You're good at this, Camille."

She ignored him and continued with her questions. "Can you at least tell me *why* you're gathering information? Is it a cheating husband? Maybe a cheating wife? Or does it have to do with theft? No one likes to think about that in this town, but it happens." She tapped a manicured finger against her small chin. "What is this about?"

The woman was nosier than a beagle on the hunt. "Do you know Jennifer Merrick?"

"Jennifer?" She scrunched her nose. "Of course I know her. Why?" When he didn't answer right away, she clasped his arm. *"Jennifer?"*

"What do you know about her?"

Camille loosened her grip on his arm, sat up straight. "Depends on why you want to know."

Her answer told him Jennifer Merrick was respected and liked and commanded a certain amount of loyalty. Jennifer's mother would be happy to hear that, no matter the outcome of this visit. Lester let out a sigh. Relationships between parents and children were tricky, especially adult children. "If Jennifer is who I think she is, then I live in the town where she grew up." He paused, measured his next words. "And I'm friends with her mother."

"Her mother?" Camille stared at him. "She's never talked about any of her relatives. Not even Hope's father."

Lester nodded. "I've got to do a little digging before I know if she's my friend's daughter. And I'll have to spend some time with her." Mimi had given him several conversations worth of details about her daughter, from her talent for cooking and baking to her love of snow and rose petals. But ten years was a long time and interests changed. Who knew what he'd find? Who knew if this was really Mimi's daughter or a false lead?

"Don't break her heart or bring her sadness." Camille's eyes glittered with tears. "Something tells me she's seen her share of both, and with a child like Hope…"

"What about her child?"

Camille let out a soft sigh. "She's different, Lester. Hope is extremely shy and doesn't like to be around people much, not

70

even kids her own age. I think her brain isn't wired like ours. Jennifer never talks about it, but I know it stresses her. What parent wants to sit by and watch her child struggle like that?" A shrug, another sigh. "The other kids don't understand her or they're afraid of her...I don't know what it is for sure. You know who Hope spends time with and isn't shy around? My brother, Oliver. Go figure. About eight months ago she started visiting Oliver's music shop and taking keyboard lessons. She came alive. When she's playing 'Benny and the Jets,' she's a different girl." Her voice splintered with emotion. "It's like a miracle."

"I'd like to meet her."

"Oh, no. Hope doesn't talk to strangers. Like I said, she doesn't talk to most of the people in town unless she's comfortable with them. She's got to trust them and she trusts Oliver. Maybe because he doesn't treat her like an oddball, or maybe because he views the world as one big joy-filled party. But I think it's because he accepts everybody and doesn't judge or try to change her. There are a lot of people in this world who say they don't judge, but you know they do. You can see it in their eyes or the set of their lips. Not Oliver." She lifted a shoulder, a smile playing about her lips. "It's hard to say exactly why he and Hope get along so well, and I've stopped guessing."

Oliver definitely sounded like someone Lester should meet. He might have a few thoughts on Jennifer Merrick, and if the man were as nonjudgmental as Camille said, then maybe he possessed the ability to remain objective, too. "Is there anything else you can tell me about Jennifer?"

Camille's smile spread. "Of course there is, but I think you should meet her and decide for yourself. If you need my help, you've got my number."

~

Rose Donovan invited Elizabeth to her home three more times. Each visit involved food, music, and stories that, while they didn't start with Rogan, always ended with him and his many attributes. They'd sat on pastel floral chairs in the enclosed porch, sipped iced tea, and commented on the gardens. A person could stare at the Donovans' back yard and never tire of the beauty or the activity found there. Elizabeth liked the screened-in back porch with its overstuffed couch and chairs. The last time she'd visited, Rose had turned on the ceiling fan because the afternoon heat threatened to be a scorcher and Rogan's mother *didn't believe in air conditioning.*

Elizabeth brought her sketchpad and worked on recreating the flowers in Rose's garden: dahlias, gerbera daisies, and zinnias, in shades of red, pink, white, and orange. But she was equally intrigued with Rogan's vegetable garden and sketched tomato plants, Brussels sprouts, lettuce, and kale. While the flowers and vegetables weren't unique to this area, they were eye-catching and, like most creative people, she couldn't pass up the opportunity to "create."

Rose told her there would be more flowers and vegetables as the summer passed and the days grew even warmer, so many, she might have to stay until fall to catch the cold crops. Elizabeth ignored the subtle hint to extend her stay in Reunion Gap, which had little to do with flowers and vegetables and everything to do with Rogan Donovan. She hadn't seen much of him, but according to his mother, he had an office on Main Street where he took care of people's taxes and gave them good advice on how to manage their money.

Rogan is very trustworthy...he's honest, humble, and kind-hearted.

He does right by others, no matter what.

Oh, but my son is intelligent. Do you know he passed his CPA exam the first time?

And after they'd spent an hour together, she'd sneak in a few more thoughts.

I don't like to see him all alone.

He's got so much to give, but he needs someone to give it to…

He could have his choice of women, but I think he's waiting for the right one…

You just never know when or how the right one will come along, do you?

You know what I think, Elizabeth? Big smile, followed by a sparkle in her eyes. *I think my son needs someone like you.*

Yes, indeed I do.

Most of what Elizabeth knew of Rogan Donovan, she'd learned from his mother or his aunt, but little had come from the man himself. Maybe it was time to seek him out. How was she ever going to right the wrongs her father had committed if she couldn't get close enough to let him see she was a decent person who wanted to help? He didn't seem like the kind of man who'd take charity, but it wasn't *charity*. It was payback for money that was stolen from his father. She had to find a way…and she would.

6

Rogan didn't like people milling around his personal space or his property, especially strangers. But that's exactly what Elizabeth Hastings had done since the first time he saw her. He'd heard all about the visits to his mother, the conversations they'd had about flowers and books, how she loved *Gone With the Wind* and soft pretzels. And his mother sure as hell made sure she told him how sincere and genuine the visitor in town was, and how maybe, if given the proper opportunity and incentive, she might want to stay in Reunion Gap.

As if he didn't know what *that* meant.

Not happening.

Just because Elizabeth Hastings had a soft spot for his mother and didn't seem to mind her offbeat ramblings did not mean Rogan had to engage in a relationship with the woman. *Why* would he do that? He didn't want a relationship that involved answering to another person, worrying you'd hurt her feelings, or worse, disappointing her by not living up to her expectations. Nope. Done with that. Unencumbered was just how he liked it.

But damn if she hadn't crept into his thoughts these past few days when his brain was relaxed. Twice, she'd even appeared in his dreams, long, blond hair brushing his shoulder, lavender scent covering him. And those lips—full, pink, moving closer…

Rogan snuffed thoughts of Elizabeth Hastings from his tired brain and concentrated on the plans in front of him. Oliver hadn't been able to make it to the plant tonight, something about working on music for Hope Merrick. He was sure involved with the kid, and the kid might not talk to most of the town, but she talked to Oliver. A lot. Not that his uncle admitted the soft spot he had for the little girl who didn't know her father and had the bad luck to be super shy. Oliver had once said everybody needed somebody, and maybe this girl filled a void for the children he didn't have.

Hard to say. It was also hard to say if his uncle's interest had anything to do with Hope's mother. Rogan hadn't missed the way he danced around the subject of Jennifer Merrick whenever her name came up, finding a way to change the conversation every single time. Yeah, that was usually a sign that went a lot deeper than *don't want to talk about it*. His uncle had a steady stream of women after him: young, old, blondes, brunettes, redheads, even a few silvers. Maybe it was the former rock-n'-roller's live-and-let-live attitude or his skill on the keyboard that attracted the women. Camille said it was the blue eyes and the soulful smile that pulled them in, but it was his ability to listen and not judge that made them want to stay. Rogan shook his head. Maybe his aunt was right, or maybe she was simply projecting traits she wished she could find in *her* husband.

Crazy.

His mother had once said his father was the kindest, gentlest man she'd ever met, filled with integrity and principles and the true desire to help others. And what had it gotten him? Too trusting, too full of integrity, too principled. All of that had landed him in the clutches of the bottle and an early death. Rogan cursed and spun his chair around to stare at the photograph of his father that rested on top of the old credenza. Dark-haired, smiling, he stood next to a sanding machine. The man had never given up his dream to run his own factory, but that dream and his honest nature had blinded him to the deceit and treachery that lived in people's souls. He sighed, stared harder at the picture. Some days, doubt crept in and made him wonder if he'd ever open the doors to this factory, or if the attempts would end in one giant disappointment. People were curious about what went on inside JD Manufacturing, and a few had the guts to ask if he really thought he'd get the place up and running again. Most just pretended it never happened and sidestepped the tragic events that led to his father's death.

Nice to have you home, Rogan.

As if he'd come home for a visit and hadn't been here two years.

You're a good boy, Rogan. Your parents must be proud.

There's only one parent left. One. The other one's dead.

Heard you helped Kyleen Gustofsen set up a spreadsheet for her card shop business. That was awful kind of you.

It's called a business plan and kind has nothing to do with it. Kyleen's father invested in JD Manufacturing and lost five thousand dollars.

"Rogan? Am I interrupting?"

He spun around, stared at the woman standing in the doorway holding a plate covered in foil. "Elizabeth? What are you doing here?"

She offered a timid smile, moved toward him and set the plate on the desk. "Your mother said you spend most evenings here, and sometimes you don't take time to eat." Another smile as she lifted the foil off the plate to reveal six plump blueberry muffins. "They're still warm," she said.

He eased a muffin off the plate, removed the paper baking

cup. "Did you make these?" He could have sworn she'd said she wasn't much good in the kitchen.

"No." She shook her head, let out a soft laugh. "Jennifer Merrick sent these."

Rogan bit into a muffin, savored the tartness. He'd heard Jennifer was a knockout cook and had the local bakery begging for her recipes, but he'd never tasted anything himself. "Delicious," he said and took another bite.

"I'll make sure to tell her you enjoyed them."

He nodded, snatched a paper towel from his desk drawer, and wiped his mouth. "We ought to get her in a cook-off challenge with Oliver. We can be the judges and we get to pick the challenges."

"Very tricky."

He stood, moved to the other side of his desk, leaned against it. "So, did you come to deliver treats, or is there another reason for the visit?" Why had she looked away when he asked her that question, as though there really *was* another reason and not one that would make him happy?

She slid her gaze to his, her expression serious. "I thought maybe you could show me this place."

He tensed. "Why? There's nothing to see but empty space."

"This empty space caused your family so much heartache, I guess I'd like to see what's left of it."

Rogan hesitated. Did he want to let this woman peek inside his personal pain? Once he let her in, he might not be able to keep her out. She could end up seeing more than the insides of a building. She might see the loss, hurt, and disappointments that were all tied up in the reason he'd returned home. It had been a long time since he'd shared anything honest with a non-family member. Did he really want to do that? Before he could question the wisdom of letting an outsider share in anything close to the truth, he nodded. "Sure. I'll take you around."

She followed him to the area where he'd been working earlier this evening, the smell of sawdust and fresh-cut wood permeating the space. Aside from Oliver and two or three others, no one had been inside the building since his father padlocked it. Rogan made his way toward the sawhorses and workbench he and his uncle had set up.

"Are you trying to renovate this place?" Elizabeth took in the equipment, the fresh sawdust, the folding chairs.

"You could say that; the operative word on the *trying*." He picked up an electrical box, studied it. "Do you have any idea how many outlets go into a place like this?" When she shook her head, he laughed. "Neither do I, but it's a lot."

She glanced at the overhead lights, the rows of pallet racks, the lumber stacked on the shelves. "There's so much to do." When he nodded, she said in a voice heaped with sympathy, "It will take forever."

He laid the box on the workbench. "It might take forever, and some days that's what it feels like, but at least Oliver's helping me."

"But when? How? You're both working, and you have your mother…"

"When you have a mission you believe in, you won't stop until it's complete. I'm doing this for my father and the life he lost." He looked away. "It can't have all been for nothing."

"I admire anyone who has such conviction and the determination to see it through," she said, her voice soft. "I don't know many people who would make such a sacrifice."

He met her gaze, willed her to understand. "My father's the one who sacrificed, and he lost. This is the only way I know to honor him." *And it's the only way to ask his forgiveness for not being there when he needed me.* That would nag Rogan for the rest of his life. If he'd not been so selfish and consumed with taking Deborah on that damned Alaskan cruise, could he have stopped the deal?

"Tell me about this place. What did it used to be like?" She glanced at the boxes of screws. "And what are your plans for it?"

The way it used to be? *That* he could talk about. He motioned her to follow him as they made their way to the front of the building and his father's old office. "All my father ever wanted was to own his own business. He was a machinist by trade, but his level head and knack for solving problems got him promoted to foreman, and then plant manager. But he was happiest when he could figure out a problem." He opened the door to a small office, waited for her to enter. "A machine problem, that is. The trickier and more complicated, the greater the challenge. When the company that was renting this place pulled out, my dad said it was an opportunity to start his own shop, and when Gordon T. Haywood came to town, my mother called it a sign. I didn't realize Dad was going to move on it so fast." He ran a hand along the desk that had belonged to his father, made a trail through the dust. "I thought there'd be more time."

"I'm so sorry."

"My father wasn't a businessman. He could run the whole place, but he didn't know about contracts, balance sheets, or taxes. He was your-handshake-is-your-word type of guy who would never cheat anyone. I'll bet Haywood saw him coming ten miles away, knew he could take whatever he wanted and all he had to do was promise to do the right thing."

"I wish someone had been there to look out for your father."

I was supposed to be there, but I failed him. "Yeah, well..."

"Will you tell me what happened to him?"

He hesitated. It had been a long time since he'd rehashed the events out loud. Thinking about them was one thing, but reliving them, especially with a stranger, was something else altogether. Elizabeth had been kind to his mother, tolerated the bold inquiries, and didn't seem to mind spending time with a woman who lived in her own world. In some odd way, he guessed he owed her and could stomach the retelling.

"My mother called me when they learned my father had been scammed. He didn't want my help, or anyone else's. He wanted to 'fix' things himself, but in the end, the only fix he found was in a bottle." *What's done is done and can't be changed*, he'd said. *Save yourself and leave me to my own devices.* "Mom couldn't cope with his drinking or his erratic behavior, and neither could my brother or sister. They both took off when I came home, and my brother hasn't been back since. My sister visits on occasion, but not much."

When Elizabeth spoke, there was no doubting the compassion in her words. "Did you have to deal with this all by yourself? I can't imagine."

Rogan shrugged. "My uncle helped out. He might look like an old-school hippie, rock-n'-roller, but he's got a big heart and a never-quit attitude. Oliver pulled me through more than once, helped me see the silver lining in a world of black."

"He reminds me of my uncle."

"Oh?" He raised a brow. "So, you have an uncle with a gray ponytail who can sing 'Stairway to Heaven' and play the keyboard, too?"

Elizabeth smiled and shook her head. "My uncle is pretty reserved. And I don't think he's much of a singer, though he did attempt 'Happy Birthday' for my sixteenth birthday, but his voice cracked and splintered before he reached the last line."

Rogan laughed. "Well, not everyone sings in the shower, the kitchen, the car...but Oliver sure does." His mood had lightened since she'd arrived and that surprised him. He'd expected the opposite, considering this place had caused so much heartache to his family. But right now, it didn't remind him of all the things that had gone wrong or had been taken from his family. Right now, it was a meeting ground for a comfortable conversation with a beautiful woman, and he was fine with that. "So, do you sing?"

She blushed crimson. "No. Absolutely not."

"Really?" That sounded like serious self-control. "How about when you've had that extra glass of wine? I'll bet you belt out a few bars of your favorite song."

The crimson turned to fuchsia. "Not even then."

"Hmm. Guess that's something we'll have to work on." He grinned and led her back to the manufacturing part of the building. "I don't have any wine here, but I've got some beer. Want one?" The look on her face said she wasn't a beer drinker, so he offered a third choice. "Or, I've got scotch." She eyed him, smiled in a way that made her amber eyes sparkle.

"I'll have a sip."

"A sip? Right."

Rogan opened the cabinet he'd installed two months ago for sandpaper and shop rags, and grabbed a bottle of scotch. He pulled out two plastic cups, uncapped the half-empty bottle and poured two healthy fingers into each cup. "Here you go," he said, handing Elizabeth a plastic cup. "And here's hoping Reunion Gap is everything you hoped it would be." They touched cups, gazes locking for a split second as a jolt surged through him that felt an awful lot like desire. *Crap.* Rogan looked away, tossed back his drink.

"My father was a scotch drinker."

He glanced at her, spotted the pain on her face, the sadness in her words. As though recalling the memory was neither welcome nor pleasant. What did he know about her family? Practically nothing, unless you counted the uncle who didn't know how to sing. But she knew quite a bit about the Donovans, almost too much if you counted tonight's sharing. He'd always made a point of keeping his feelings inside, but he'd broken the rules with Elizabeth Hastings.

Why was that?

Because she'd been kind to his mother, shown her patience and actual interest? Because she'd brought him blueberry muffins even though she hadn't baked them? Or was it those amber eyes and full lips that pulled him in, made him want to explore her secrets, taste her, touch her… He stared into his cup, wondered how many of these it would take to block out Elizabeth's voice, the curve of her neck… Was her skin as soft as it looked? Softer?

"Rogan?"

He looked up, lost himself in those eyes. "Yes?" The idea of kissing her was absurd and out of line, especially for someone who'd vowed he wanted nothing to do with relationships. This woman wasn't a one-night stand or a weekly hookup; she was commitment and long-term. She was for keeps. Rogan cleared his throat, stepped back.

"Thank you." She closed the distance between them, touched his arm. "For sharing. I know you'll reopen this place and honor your father." Her voice spilled over him. "I want to help."

Caution snuffed out the desire he'd felt a few seconds ago. "Help? How would you help?"

"I'd like to invest in the company."

"No." Rogan shrugged off her hand. "I appreciate the offer, but I don't really know you. No offense, but just because we've shared a few meals and talked, you're a stranger." His gaze narrowed on her. "And you should consider me a stranger, too. How do you know I won't cheat you out of your money, like that guy did to my father?"

"I trust you," she said in a quiet voice.

"Yeah, well, you shouldn't. You don't know me. You don't know anything about me."

Her eyes grew bright. "I know you're kind. And honest."

He sighed. "That is the absolute worst reason to partner with someone. You don't invest in a person's business because you think they're kind and honest." Another sigh, this one deeper, louder. "You invest because you're going to get a decent return, as in, make money."

"But what if it's about more than money? What if I want to help realize a dead man's dream, a man who's been wronged?" Her voice dipped, wobbled. "How could that possibly be a bad idea?"

"Because then I'd be beholden to you." Rogan poured another drink, tossed it back and set the plastic cup on the counter next to him. "And that's a problem."

"Because it's me, or wouldn't you take help from anybody?"

There was a hell of a lot of emotion in that question. "That depends. I'd have to ask myself if there were a catch and what strings were attached, because it's never a clean-cut deal. I like negotiating with banks rather than friends: much easier, less emotion. Besides—" he scratched his jaw "—your business reasoning makes no sense." He could tell she didn't like that last comment by the way her lips thinned and she let out a tiny huff, as though trying not to lose her temper.

"Everything in life and business is not about the bottom line." Another huff, accompanied by what could almost be classified as a scowl. "My father spent his life chasing money, justifying his actions because it was all for my future. At least that's what he said every time he missed a school event or a chance for family time. He never considered how lonely I was, or that I needed a father more than a fat bank account." Her gaze grew brighter, her words bolder. "All of that money will never replace the memories I lost out on because of it. You think I'm not good at business because I make decisions with my heart? You'd rather see me bring an accountant along and pull out spreadsheets and a calculator? I'm not interested in that, Rogan. I see a chance to make a difference, to invest in a good person—you—and I don't care if it takes thirty years to recoup my money. *What I care about* is helping you and your family realize a dream that was stolen from you by a man who had no right to do that." Her lips quivered with her next words. "I don't know if I'll ever have an opportunity to invest in anything as rewarding as this again. Please, let me do this; let me help undo the wrong this man committed against your family and give all of you a second chance."

What to say to that? Thank you? No thank you? It was the most selfless thing he'd ever heard.

"Rogan?"

"I don't know. Since the moment I saw you, you've confused me. I need time to think and a clear head, neither of which I seem capable of when you're around." Damn, had he really just admitted *that*? "I'll be in touch."

LESTER CONROY HAD BEEN uncovering people's secrets for years, and one conversation with the proprietor of the Peace & Harmony Inn told him the woman had a secret. There were the obvious signs: the hesitation when he asked about her family, the darting gaze that couldn't quite meet his, the fidgeting. And if those weren't sure signs of avoidance and hiding-something-I-don't-want-to-talk-about, Jennifer Merrick had a habit of rubbing her forefinger and thumb together in tiny circles when Lester dumped a question on her she didn't want to answer.

Yup, the woman was covering up something, and he'd bet his Stetson *and* his cowboy boots that something had to do with her family. He'd gone easy on her during their first chat, complimented her on the inn, told her he was a Texan but admired small-town life. Chit-chat that made a person's defenses slip if they were talking to a stranger. No question about family. He saved that for their second chat, slid it right in between the cherry pie she offered him and his second cup of coffee.

Did I mention I was a grandfather? Inherited a couple kids and grandkids when I got married last year. Never thought I'd see the day when I'd sit on the floor with blocks or roll out Play-Doh. One of the girls is teaching me a new dance. I didn't realize how much I was missing until those kids came into my life. Grandkids can make a person humble, but some days they make me feel like king of the world. He'd cut her the eye, paused. *You probably hear that from Hope's grandparents all the time.*

A hard blink and then a quiet, *Actually, I don't.*

How so?

A sucked-in breath, followed by a clipped, *Hope doesn't know her grandparents.*

Hmm. Sorry about that. Have they...passed on?

A shake of that dark head. *I have no idea. Now, can we please change the subject? This is not a particularly pleasant topic.*

Imagine not, and I meant no offense. I'm real sorry, Jennifer.

There'd been no more talk of grandparents or children being the bright spot in their lives. Lester steered the topics to places he'd visited and what he'd seen: the Badlands of South Dakota, the Carlsbad Caverns of New Mexico, and a whole lot in his home state of Texas. He didn't mention the area where he'd settled, the one he loved most of all, Magdalena, New York, because that was where Mimi Pendergrass's daughter had been born and raised, and that's where her mother still lived.

If he still had the gambling habits of his younger days, he'd bet his last dollar Jennifer Merrick had been Jennifer Pendergrass. The question wasn't how to prove it because he'd been in this line of work long enough to have a gut feeling about people and situations. He'd get that answer soon enough and wouldn't have to work too hard to do it. The real question was not even *why* Jennifer left Magdalena and broke it off with her parents. Nope, none of that mattered, or at least not as much as the one that could change lives: *did* Jennifer want to make amends with her mother?

That was the center of everything, the beginning of a new life or the end of an old one, and nobody could answer that question but Jennifer. That's where the third conversation came in, the one they were having at this very moment, and the one she was less than thrilled about.

"Mr. Conroy, would you like another slice of rye toast?"

Lester held up a hand. "No, but thank you. I sure did enjoy that mushroom and Swiss omelet. I think it was as good as the one my wife makes, but I could never tell her. Wouldn't want to hurt her feelings." He folded his napkin, placed it on the table. "We do a lot to protect the people we love, don't we?"

Jennifer picked up his plate, carried it to the sink. "Yes, we do."

He couldn't see her face, but the tone in her voice said sad and maybe he'd heard a tinge of regret, too. "I got myself into a terrible situation a few years back. Told a tale and my wife believed it. She wasn't my wife then, and if the good Lord hadn't seen fit to give me a second chance, she wouldn't be my wife now. But she forgave me, and so did the rest of the town." Lester sat back in his chair, crossed his arms over his belly. "I never meant to hurt anybody and at the time, I was just doing my job. How did I know the people in that town would become friends, or the waitress who served up my coffee and pie would take a shine to me, and I'd feel the same about her?"

Jennifer turned to face him, leaned against the counter, her expression guarded but curious. "What did you do?"

"Almost ruined a town, almost caused a divorce between one of the best couples I know. And she was pregnant, too." He shook his head, the omelet he'd just eaten bouncing in his belly. "You're wondering why I'd do such a thing, aren't you?" When she nodded, he let out a breath, forced the memories to slow down. "I thought I was just doing my job, like I was paid to do, but what started out as an investigation of a woman's husband turned into something evil and I was part of it. I'll always be part of that and no matter how much good I try to do for those people, I have to live with the bad I did, too." Lester eyed her, spoke in a rough voice full of the hurts he'd caused his friends. "Do you know why I'm here, Jennifer?" She shook her head, clasped her hands around her middle. "I promised my wife I'd try to help a person in need. You see, this woman does a lot of good for the town, never complains even when you know she's seen her share of grief. Lost a husband to illness, a son to a car accident, and a daughter to angry words and a ton of regret."

Jennifer had gone pale, her lips white, eyes wide. Was she shaking? Hard to tell from Lester's position, but it sure looked like it. "The loss of the daughter is what eats at her; you can see it in my friend's eyes when she looks at a dark-haired young woman in her mid-thirties." He paused, rubbed his jaw. "About your age."

"Stop," she whispered, squeezing her eyes shut. "Please."

"Your mother misses you, Jennifer. There's a hole in her heart and nobody can fill it but you."

Her eyes flew open and she advanced on him, fists clenched, mouth a slash of fury. "How dare she send you here! You know nothing about me or what happened."

"No, I sure don't." He stood, moved toward her. "That's not my business, and it's not why I'm here. I've only come to see if there's a chance you can reconcile." These next words hurt to say, but he'd promised his wife and he wouldn't break that promise. "If you can't, if the hurt is so deep you'll never find your way out, then I'll leave and you won't hear from me again." He picked up his hat, held it between his hands. "If that's the case, I'll head back to Magdalena and tell your mother you're alive and well, running a bed-and-breakfast that reminds me of hers. I'll even tell her about Hope, but I won't mention the name you're using or why, and I sure as the devil won't tell her about the anger I see on your face right now. I can't do that to Mimi. I'll say you've moved on."

"Moved on? You have no idea."

"No, I don't, but I've walked this earth long enough to realize that there comes a time when you have to accept your part in what goes wrong. You can't blame the world and everybody in it for what's not working for you. At some point, that's on you. I worked for a woman who wanted everyone including her own daughter to pay for the way her life turned out. You know what happened to her? She died without her family, and the only person at her side was a paid companion. I don't want that for you, Jennifer. Fix things with your mother or don't, but stop blaming her for the parts of your life that haven't worked out. If you don't, you're going to end up all alone." He plopped his Stetson on his head, said in a soft voice, "And I mean all alone. You think on it. I'll be here another day or two and then I'm heading home."

7

Rogan knew he was in trouble when he cancelled his Thursday night "meeting" with Alyssa. He'd cancelled last Thursday, too, but that hadn't had anything to do with Elizabeth Hastings's presence in Reunion Gap. At least that's what he told himself, and for the most part, he'd been able to believe it. But when Alyssa called to tell him she'd booked dinner reservations at the cozy Italian restaurant he favored, with a promise of "dessert" afterward at her place, he'd worked up an excuse to decline. The tightness in her voice told him she didn't like that response, and she'd countered with questions, too many for the no-strings relationship they'd both said they wanted.

Was he the only one who meant what he said?

He'd apologized because he didn't want to get into an argument with her, not when he had too many other issues pounding his brain. Rogan might not be a relationship guru like Oliver, but Alyssa's reaction to his two-weeks-in-a-row cancellation said she was way more invested in him than she'd let on.

And that was a problem.

Even if Elizabeth Hastings hadn't walked into town with her fresh-faced-girl-next-door attitude, he would've cut ties with

Alyssa. Why let her think there would ever be anything more between them than the no-commitment sex and good times they'd shared these past few months? Her reaction to his cancellation told him she thought there could be, or worse, thought there already *was* more to them than Thursday night sex.

And that brought him back to Elizabeth. He'd pondered her offer for three long days, and finally come up with an answer. Well, maybe it wasn't a clear-cut yes or no, but it was a path to an answer, and right now that was the best he could do. If she accepted his offer, they'd see where life took them. If she didn't… Rogan pushed that thought from his mind, picked up the phone and dialed her number.

"Meet me at the plant tonight. Eight-thirty."

Pause. "I thought you didn't work Thursday nights."

Thanks to his mother, Elizabeth knew a bit too much about him. What she meant was that he wasn't working because he had other plans on Thursdays that involved a mystery woman in another town. And sex. Lots of sex. Rogan cleared his throat, said, "From now on, Thursday nights are open."

"Oh. I see."

Yeah, the softness in her voice was all female and spoke of definite approval. If he were a weaker guy, he'd be lapping up the approval like a thirsty puppy. But he wasn't a pup and he damn well wasn't weak. "See you tonight," he said, annoyed that he'd revealed a bit too much about the fate of his Thursday nights, and worse, the reason behind it.

Elizabeth arrived at JD Manufacturing at eight-twenty, dressed in a navy blouse and jeans, her blonde hair brushing her arms. He wondered about that hair, guessed it would be soft and silky and smell like the lavender scent she wore. But wondering wasn't knowing…

"Hello, Rogan."

He tossed his pencil on the workbench, nodded. "Elizabeth."

She worked up a smile. "It's been a long three days."

"You have no idea." He'd battled with logic, judgment, instinct, and every other skill he'd employed in the past when caught in such a dilemma. But Elizabeth Hastings made logic, judgment, *and* instinct difficult to quantify.

"That bad?"

When she smiled, her face lit up, pulled out the dimples on either side of her mouth. "Bad," he nodded, returning the smile. "Horrible bad." He snatched the bottle of scotch resting on the workbench. "The kind that requires a little help to see through the fog." Rogan poured two fingers in a plastic cup, then filled a second. "To the future of JD Manufacturing."

She accepted her cup, saluted him. "To the future."

They sipped their scotch, made small talk about the weather, the blueberry muffins, and his mother's latest matchmaking pitch. Rogan refilled their drinks, tried not to think about the conversation looming between them. Soon, he'd have to bring it up, and then he'd have to tell her his decision. She could either accept it, and they'd move forward, or reject it, and they'd be pretty much done on all levels. Dread shot to his throat, inched out. "So, I guess we should talk about the proposal." He didn't want to talk about the proposal or anything else right now. All he wanted to do was sip scotch with a beautiful woman and enjoy the moment.

Was that really too much to ask?

She set her cup on the bench, met his gaze. "I guess we should." Pause, a lick of her glossy lips. "Look, Rogan, I'm not trying to push you or make you do anything you don't want to do. Whatever happens has to be your call." She bit her bottom lip. "I offered to help for the reasons I stated, but I know you're a proud man and I respect that. You're also a man of honor who wants to do the right thing. That's a trait you don't see much these days, not when many people take short cuts that are one-sided and self-serving. Whatever your decision, I'll accept it."

Those amber eyes glittered as she waited for his answer. She was so damn beautiful and so damn tempting.

Too tempting.

He closed the distance between them, cupped her face with his hands, and kissed her. The kiss was gentle, hesitant at first… until she opened her mouth and their tongues touched. Scotch and desire blended, turned the kiss hot, deep, needy. Rogan slid his hands along her back, pulled her to him, forgetting all the reasons they should *not* be doing this. The woman had distracted him since the first time he saw her. Hadn't he known deep down that sooner or later, he'd have to taste her, and once he did, it would not be enough? He'd want more. He'd want her—all of her. Rogan backed her up against the work table. "Elizabeth," he murmured, breaking the kiss to drag his lips along her jaw, her neck, the opening of her shirt. He unfastened the first button, then the second, eased the fabric aside to expose a pink lace bra. "Pink lace. My new favorite."

He traced the rim of her bra, saw the desire in her eyes. But there was something else there, too. *Vulnerability.* Elizabeth trusted him not to take advantage of her. That's not what he was doing. *Was it?* Of course not. Whatever was about to happen was consensual, aimed at pure enjoyment, without regard for a deeper involvement. His hand stilled. *Who was he kidding?* Elizabeth wasn't a one-and-done kind of woman. She'd want a commitment, maybe the forever kind. Was he ready for that? Rogan eased the fabric over her bra, fastened the buttons. *The truth?* He didn't know, and until he figured it out, he couldn't touch her.

"Rogan? What's wrong?" She reached out, clasped his hand.

"The truth?"

Her brows pinched together. "I always want you to tell me the truth. No matter what."

He sighed, squeezed her hand. "I had a different life when I lived in California. Fancy dinners, clubs…a fiancée. When I told her I planned to come back to Reunion Gap to help my folks, she said 'thanks but no thanks.' I guess I thought when you were in a relationship, especially on the verge of marriage, you were all in, no matter what." Rogan stared at their joined hands, shrugged. "And then I learned that wasn't necessarily true. Some people were in the relationship as long as it was convenient, or maybe as long as it wasn't inconvenient. Once it got difficult, they bailed." He slid his gaze to hers. "That's what happened to me, and from that moment on, I didn't want long-term or anything close to a relationship. *I* became the one who wanted convenient. No strings, no questions, no expectations."

Elizabeth's eyes grew bright. "I'm sorry someone hurt you. I've never been able to let anyone get close enough to hurt me." She shrugged. "Giving another person that kind of control petrifies me."

"I know, but what I'm realizing is that there's no guarantee in this world. You can do everything right and your life could still land on top of you. But even if that happens, at least you've known a few moments of happiness." He paused, brought her hand to his lips, kissed it. "At least you've lived."

Her voice turned breathy, her words unsure. "What are you trying to say?"

"I don't know anything about you, and I can't do a deal with someone I don't know." He worked up a smile. "The kissing and touching wasn't part of the deal. That's something else altogether."

"It is?"

He tried to force the heat from his face, failed. "If you want it to be."

She touched his cheek, trailed a finger to his jaw. "I like the sound of that."

Rogan clasped her hand, held it. "There's the business deal, and then—" he paused, placed a soft kiss on the underside of her wrist that made her sigh "——there's the personal deal. Mutually exclusive, but apt to intersect at times." Another kiss, this one in the palm of her hand. "Business-wise, I've got to know more about you before I can even think about your offer. Where did you grow up? What have you been doing these past several years? It's going to take time; I'm a very cautious businessperson. On the personal end, what makes you happy? Hell, I don't know; maybe, what do you eat for breakfast?" She sniffed and a tear slipped down her cheek, landed on her blouse. "Hey, this wasn't supposed to make you cry. I want to get to know you, Elizabeth Hastings, because I think there's something between us, or could be." He leaned toward her, brushed his lips against hers. "I haven't felt that way in a long time, and I don't want to screw it up by moving too fast."

She eased back, studied him. "You mean sleeping together."

"Right." Sure, he was dying to get into bed with her; what guy wouldn't be? But then what? He'd had enough of the sex-now-questions-later type of hook-ups to know they wouldn't last past the first step out of bed. That's not what he wanted with Elizabeth. He wanted trust, and commitment, and a feeling of belonging.

"So, sleeping together is off limits?" she said in a voice that made him think of sex and lots of it.

"For now."

She flung her arms around his neck, a smile bursting from those beautiful lips. "That's the perfect answer. Too bad you've sworn off sex because words like that make a girl *want* to have sex with you."

Rogan stared at her, tried to figure out if she were teasing or half-serious. From the way she licked her bottom lip, he'd say a little of both. "I said no sex; I didn't say no to everything in between." He pulled her close, kissed her long and hard, let the passion flow between them. It felt so right and so damn good to be with her. When she moved against him, he cursed the damn conscience that wanted to get to know her before they had sex. And when her tongue teased his and those little moans escaped her lips? Well, that made him hot, ready, and about to change his mind on the sex part.

But he didn't because this woman was worth the wait. Of course, the more time they spent together, the more they'd learn about each other, and the shorter the wait. Yeah, he liked the sound of that. Rogan trailed his tongue along her neck, sucked. Two weeks should do it, three tops, and once he got her in bed, he might not let her out.

HARRISON ALEXANDER HAD MONEY, power, and friends in high places. He'd always liked the fact that people were afraid of him, including his own family, especially his wife, Marguerite. She died six years ago, the result of what doctors called complications of a weak heart, but everybody knew that while her heart might have stopped, it was her husband who decided it was time for it to quit ticking. Oh, he didn't kill her, not outright. A man like that didn't have to get his hands dirty. When a person's usefulness was done, Harrison discarded them, and they either withered away or combusted. In Marguerite's case, the barrage of demeaning remarks, the stream of mistresses, the whispers of illegitimate children, and the dirty dealings had taken a toll on the genteel woman from Virginia.

Enough was enough.

The town mourned the loss of the delicate Southerner who never uttered an unkind word against her husband or any other living creature. No indeed, Marguerite kept it all inside, year after year, until one day, she simply ceased to exist. Her children cried. Angry and desperate, they'd been unable to convince their mother to leave the man who'd been more tyrant than husband or father.

She could have found moments of peace, could have enjoyed her grandchildren one day.

She could have been happy.

But she refused.

Marguerite believed in marriage until death and it was this belief that killed her one sunny morning in late May, snuffed out her breath while she slept alone in the master bedroom. Her husband had dispensed of her years ago, deemed her insignificant and useless. What he'd failed to consider was the affect her death would have on their children. Perhaps he'd not thought of this because he didn't *understand* his children, or perhaps because he'd never quite understood his wife's importance in the Alexander family. Marguerite was the one her children loved; she was the one the hired help listened to when Harrison finished his latest tirade.

Losing her meant losing the one person who kept order in the family and in the household. When Marguerite died, so did the tolerance for a father who'd treated his children and his wife as possessions. The eldest, Tate, was the first to defect, leaving town the same day as his mother's funeral. He headed to Chicago where he teamed up with a real estate development company and vowed never to set foot in Reunion Gap again. Neal hung around just long enough to get a chunk of inheritance money before he flew to Australia with his latest bedmate. His twin sister, Meredith, tried to stay and run the household, but the idea and the implementation proved disastrous. She left for an undisclosed location five days after Neal.

Life trudged along for six years with occasional visits from Meredith and short stays from Neal, usually when the boy needed more money. Tate remained true to his word and did not return to Reunion Gap. No one knew if the eldest son's decision to stay away caused Harrison Alexander pain, though many wondered how it could when the man possessed no feelings, and the presence of a heart was questionable.

But what they didn't know and wouldn't know for years was that Tate Livingstone Alexander was the one person his father admired, and the one he'd chosen as successor to HA Properties, Inc.

TATE ALEXANDER LEFT Reunion Gap the same day as his mother's funeral. He would have kept good on his promise never to return if his old man weren't lying in a hospital bed, the victim of lifestyle choices and an unlucky genetics pool. Or maybe it was the ruthlessness of a man who possessed no soul that had finally taken him down, paralyzed his right side, stolen his speech. Doctors didn't know about the length or degree of his recovery, nobody did, but Tate bet most of the town was waiting to find out, probably wishing the old man never made it out of that hospital bed.

The Alexanders might own most of Reunion Gap, but it was no secret Harrison Alexander had followed his father's footsteps and cheated, lied, stolen, and betrayed a lot of people to gain such wealth. It didn't matter what they had to do to get a strip of land or an agreement; if they wanted it, they found a way to get it. They were cheaters, swindlers, and double-dealers who escaped the sins of their deeds every single time. Tate hated growing up an Alexander, hated the stigma, the threat associated with his name, the knowledge that no matter how he tried to make things right, he would be judged by his father's and his grandfather's deeds. His mother had not been strong enough to fight the inevitable will of a man who believed his family was his property and she'd given up, slipped away in her sleep one morning, as quiet in death as she'd been in life.

When the long-time company lawyer called four days ago to tell him about his father's stroke, Tate had been working on a land development deal with his business partner.

Your father's had a stroke, Tate. A rather serious one.

Sorry to hear that, Frederick.

We need you to come home and run the business until he's well enough to resume these responsibilities himself.

Again, sorry to hear about my father, but I can't help you out. My home and my business are in Chicago.

The company needs you, Tate. Your father was very specific that if something happened to him, you would run the company.

You think that was guilt talking? Oh, sorry, I forgot. Couldn't be guilt because my father doesn't have a conscience.

Tate, please. He always knew you were the one he could count on to do the right thing. Will you come home? We can't let your brother get involved. It would be a disaster.

Neal in charge? Disaster's an understatement. What about Meredith? She could handle it.

He wanted you, Tate. Don't let your personal feelings ruin this company.

Personal feelings, huh? That's an interesting way to summarize loathing and disgust for the man who fathered me.

You'd have full control.

Full control?

Yes. Can I count on you?

I'll see you in three days.

And now, here he was, back in the town he swore he'd never set foot in again. Life had a way of twisting promises, forcing a person to break them, no matter how well intentioned the initial promise was. He'd been called home to run the family business, or maybe he should call HA Properties, Inc., the family empire, because Harrison Alexander owned hundreds of hotels up and down the East Coast as well as investment real estate that extended across the country. Word had it his brother was gallivanting in Palm Springs with a singer from Buenos Aires, and the family residence was empty. Thank God. He wouldn't have minded seeing his sister, but she'd visited him in Chicago last month before heading to who knew where to teach people how to grow their own food. Meredith wanted to save the world, one Brussels sprout at a time, a trait he was certain their father detested. *Never show you care too much*, the old man had bellowed. *It's a weakness and Alexanders aren't weak.*

Harrison Alexander had a lot of other sayings that had burrowed in Tate's head, screwed him up, and made him question why he couldn't have a normal relationship. He thought of the one woman who made him feel almost normal. She gave him hope, made him think he didn't have to spend his whole life on the outside of a relationship.

Too bad she despised him.

"Mr. Tate! Welcome home."

A round, gray-haired woman rushed toward him, arms outspread, smile covering her heart-shaped face. Astrid Long-house had been the Alexanders' cook since he was old enough to find his way to the kitchen for chocolate chip cookies and milk. "How's my favorite chef?" She blushed when he called her that, said she was nothing of the sort, but nobody could fix a better chateaubriand or lemon cheesecake than Astrid. What was a title anyway? Just words that didn't mean anything if you couldn't back them up with the real deal. Tate hugged her, gave her a kiss on the cheek that made her blush.

"It's so good to have you home again, Mr. Tate." Her dark eyes filled with tears, her words coated with sadness. "It has not been the same since Mrs. Alexander passed." More tears, accompanied by sniffs and a sign of the cross. "We have all waited for your return."

By *all* she meant Benny, Millie, Tom, and Astrid: the gardener, cleaning lady, repairman, and herself. Tate had always preferred their company to the pain-in-the-butt stuck-ups his father tried to foist on him. He'd liked real people with real-life situations, not ones who pretended to be what they weren't— better than everybody else. That's why he'd liked Rogan Donovan, had buddied up with him, competed in sports and academics, until Tate's old man stepped in and made sure his son came out on top of every competition. Of course, Tate hadn't found out until the trust was broken and Rogan Donovan believed he was as corrupt as the rest of the Alexanders.

But the end came one summer, right before senior year, with a lie that turned Rogan against him for good, and a truth that would remain hidden for years. Tate never did find out how the rumors started or why Rogan's girlfriend was at the center of it. He had his ideas, though, and they started and ended with Harrison Alexander and a big, fat payoff.

"Your room is ready, Mr. Tate, and I've fixed your favorite for tonight's meal." She paused, her face lighting up as she recited the menu. "Chicken cordon bleu, mashed potatoes, broccoli-cheese bake, and a chocolate cake for dessert."

He didn't eat that many carbs in a month, and he hadn't had a potato in two years. But if Astrid wanted to please him with his "favorite" meal, then he would not disappoint her. Tate worked up a smile, said in a gentle voice, "Thank you for the welcome home dinner, Astrid. I take it I'll be dining alone?"

She bit her bottom lip, nodded. "Unless you would like me to extend an invitation to someone." Her thin lips pulled into a smile. "A young woman perhaps?"

He laughed. "You give me too much credit. I haven't been in

Reunion Gap for more than ten minutes, so I'm a little light in the female companionship area."

The woman cocked a brow as if to say, *You don't fool me, Tate Alexander, even though you might fool the rest of the world.* "Is that so?"

Why was she looking at him like that? "Is there something you want to say?" They'd played this game since he'd been old enough to understand that silence often held answers, if a person only looked for them. Astrid never made it easy for him when she was trying to steer him toward answers and truths he might not want to face. A raised brow, a comment, a faint hum. "Astrid?"

She moved toward him, placed a hand on his shirtsleeve, and said in a soft voice, "She'll be home soon. I thought you'd want to know." Then she patted his arm and headed toward the kitchen, leaving him in the foyer, thinking about her words.

There was no need to ask who *she* was, because they both knew her name, knew too that what he felt for her must remain a secret, at least for now. Maybe forever.

8

"Why did my father put me in charge of the company when I've barely spoken to him in six years?" Tate eased into the big leather chair that belonged to his father, picked up a paperweight with the words *The Alleghenies* scrawled over it. "And I want the truth, Fred, not some BS about how much he needs me."

Frederick Strong settled his thin frame into the plush chair across from Tate. The man looked like a child in a suit, his boyish face and sandy curls making him appear ten years younger than his fifty-some years. And the brain in that boyish body? That was pure genius. Some said the reason HA Properties, Inc., had not only been able to stay afloat in rocky times, but flourish and expand. One way or another, Frederick was behind the push to bring Tate home.

"The company needs new blood, Tate." Frederick adjusted his horn-rimmed glasses, studied him. "You're that new blood."

"Me? Because I'm an Alexander?"

"Because when you speak, people listen." Frederick gripped the arms of the chair, sat up straight. "People *want* to listen to you. Not because they fear you or fear retribution, but because they believe in you." He curled his right hand into a ball, thumped the arm of the chair. "We need leadership like that, and with your father in a less than ideal physical state right now, this is the perfect time to align you with the rest of the owners."

Last he knew, his father was the majority owner, with a few of his friends holding minor, insignificant shares in the company. "Why would I need to align myself with anybody other than my father?" He rubbed his jaw, spotted the splash of red coloring the man's cheeks and wondered what Frederick hadn't told him.

The man who'd been his father's legal advisor and friend—if Harrison Alexander had friends—shifted in his chair, darted a glance at the desk, and fixed his gaze in the vicinity of Tate's tie. "There was a shift a few years back." He paused, cleared his throat. "Your father made some...questionable decisions and in order to set them aside, he had to give up significant shares."

What the hell was he talking about? What questionable decisions? Everything the old man did was a questionable decision. Was he talking illegal? And how large were significant shares? "How about translating that for me, Fred. I'm not following unless you're referring to some sort of illegal activity."

The man's face turned to paste, his eyes grew wide behind the glasses, and he coughed. Once, twice, three times before he rasped, "Exactly."

Damn it. He'd suspected his father of ruthless behavior and questioned the ethical nature of some of his dealings, but he'd never thought the man would dip into illegal activities. It must have been bad if he'd given up a portion of his company. Tate sighed. "What did he do?"

Frederick's eyes grew wider, his voice raspier. "Leave it alone, Tate. It's best you don't know. Sleeping dogs and all that." He cleared his throat, said in a steadier voice, "Suffice it to say, the board has chosen you over your father, at least until your father has recovered. At that point, we'll see what happens."

"Why couldn't you just tell me that when you called? You didn't think I should know what was happening?" Harrison Alexander was no longer majority shareholder of HA Properties, Inc.? Hard to believe.

"The board thought it best to bring you in before presenting their offer."

Tate laughed. "Oh, they did, huh? Who's on this board?" He'd known the whole town before he left, the likeables and the unlikeables, the trustworthy and the not-so-trustworthy.

Frederick shot him a look, said in an even voice, "There are seven on the board. I'll get you the list." A long pause, before he added, "You'll have the opportunity to meet them tomorrow morning, 9:00 a.m." His lips pulled into a faint smile. "They're all quite excited to meet you." The smile spread. "This is going to be a very good thing for you, Tate, you'll see."

GETTING to know Rogan Donovan and *not* landing in bed with him was a challenge. It wasn't that she slept around, but there was something about the man that pulled her in, made her want to be with him in a very physical way. When he talked about a relationship the other night, it had scared her. She'd never let anyone get that close, had always been on the outside from the time she was a child, watching her parents.

It was all about trust.

Could she trust Rogan Donovan not to hurt her? Could she trust him enough to share memories of the insecure, lonely girl she'd been? And most of all, would there come a time when she could tell him who she really was, and more importantly, who her father was?

It had been two days since she'd met him at JD Manufacturing. Two days since they'd kissed, touched, admitted they had feelings for one another, feelings that, if nurtured, might grow and turn into a commitment. Or something close. What did that mean exactly? Love? Marriage? Children?

Did she want that?

When she was around Rogan, the answer was clear. Yes, she absolutely did! But when she was alone, memories of the little girl whose parents could not find enough love in their hearts to include her, resurfaced. Was she not loveable? Rogan wanted her to open up to him but could she do it? Could she risk that hurt again?

She pulled up in front of Oliver Donovan's place, parked the SUV, and grabbed the container of double fudge brownies Rose had baked this morning. Apparently, these were Oliver's favorites and he'd insisted nobody could make a double fudge brownie like his sister-in-law. Elizabeth climbed the stairs to the music shop and opened the door. "Oliver?"

"Just a minute," he called from the other room.

Elizabeth set the brownies on the counter, noticed a small stack of books on a shelf. *Catcher in the Rye, The Great Gatsby, The Prophet*. From their first meeting, she'd known Oliver Donovan was more than he let on to be. Nobody spoke to a child with such gentleness or took the time to explain sharps and flats if he didn't possess compassion and understanding. But it had been more than that. The man actually seemed to *care* about Hope, and if the dip in his voice when he mentioned Hope's mother were any indication, he cared about Jennifer, too. Oliver Donovan and Jennifer Merrick—an unlikely couple at first glance, who might not be so unlikely at all.

She pictured Uncle Everett at the keyboard dressed in a suit and tie, monogrammed shirt starched, handkerchief folded in his breast pocket. He would be a sight next to Oliver Donovan. The man probably didn't own a suit or a tie, and certainly didn't get his hair trimmed every three weeks, whether it needed it or not. And singing? She'd bet Oliver not only sang but wrote the lyrics, too.

"Hey, Elizabeth." Oliver Donovan made his way out of the back room, laughed when he spotted the container in front of her. "Let me guess. Double fudge brownies from my sister-in-law?"

Elizabeth nodded. "How'd you know?"

He unsnapped the lid, lifted out a brownie. "Rose's been trying to beat my recipe for double fudge brownies since the day she and Jonathan got hitched." He bit into the brownie, chewed. "Good stuff, but not as good as mine."

"But that's not what she said." Elizabeth frowned. "She said you loved her brownies, and there was nobody who could make them like her."

Another laugh, a shake of his ponytail. "She said that, huh?"

"She did." Elizabeth paused, the frown deepened. "With great emotion."

Oliver popped the rest of the brownie in his mouth, pointed to the container. "She's almost caught up to me, but she knows she's not quite there yet. Back in the day, we used to line up Jonathan and the kids, blindfold them, and let them taste-test our brownies." He grinned, reached for another one. "I beat her every time. She used to huff around, wanting a recall or some other silliness. We sure had a good time with it." His expression turned serious, his voice thick with emotion. "That was a long time ago."

She knew he meant before the business deal that crushed his brother. "I'm so sorry." If she could get Rogan to agree to let her help him finance the business, maybe the family would find peace knowing JD Manufacturing would open and operate as Jonathan intended. But Rogan insisted those discussions were not happening right now. She wished she'd met him under different circumstances, where they could be simply two people interested and curious to know one another. Instead, she had her father's deviousness sitting square in the middle of whatever might develop between them.

How would she ever tell Rogan who she really was, who her father was?

"Have you seen the rangy Texan strolling about town in his Stetson and cowboy boots?" Oliver asked. "He's staying at the Peace & Harmony Inn, so you might have run into him?"

"Rangy Texan?" She'd been too busy thinking about her predicament and Rogan Donovan to notice. How did a person *not* notice a Texan in a place like Reunion Gap? Preoccupation with other things, that's how. "No, I must've missed him. Why do you ask?"

Oliver rubbed his stubbled jaw, leaned against the counter. "Just curious. I hear he's an investigator."

"An investigator?"

"Uh-huh. Interesting, isn't it?"

"Maybe he's just visiting." The possibility sounded weak and implausible, even to her. Who was this investigator and why was he here? Had Uncle Everett sent him? If so, why would he do that? Hadn't he told her the investigator had a person from Reunion Gap reporting back to him? Maybe she should talk to Jennifer, see what she could find out. She'd call Uncle Everett, too. She didn't need any outside interference, not when she was trying to gain Rogan's trust and work on whatever else might be happening between them...

"Elizabeth?"

"Yes?"

Those blue eyes narrowed on her. "Why is it you know so much about everybody in this town?" Oliver sat on the stool behind the counter, crossed his arms over his chest. "I've been listening to you and I'm surprised at how much you know about the people here." The smile faded. "Rose talks, but she doesn't dive in deep unless it's about Jonathan or the kids. But you know almost as much as I do and I've lived here a good part of my life."

Stay calm. Don't let him see he's unnerved you. Elizabeth tilted her head as though considering his question, when she knew exactly what she'd tell him—even when it was only part of the truth. "I've got a curious nature, I guess. My mother used to tell me I was destined to be a reporter because of my inquisitive nature, but I chose art instead." Yes, her mother had made comments about the endless questions, but they hadn't been kind.

He nodded, his brows pinched together. "Are you really here to draw the flora and fauna? Or is there another reason?" He scratched his stubbled jaw, studied her. "People have a fascination with small towns. They think they're places to go where you can pull up a chair, have a cup of coffee, a slice of homemade pie, and get asked to join the garden club. Reunion Gap isn't like that. We don't tell tales to strangers until they become friends, and it's darn hard for *that* to happen in a town that's extra cautious about outsiders."

She sipped in a breath, forced out bits of half-truths. "I'm here to draw and enjoy small-town life. I've been to other places, much smaller than Reunion Gap, and the people have been open and welcoming." Another bit of half-truth. She'd been on *vacation* in tiny villages, and what resort wouldn't welcome a tourist who spent good amounts of money there? "What happened to make this town so distrustful?" Was her father the real reason for the distrust, or had his actions further confirmed the town's belief that a stranger could never be trusted?

"What didn't happen?" Oliver reached for his water bottle, tapped it on his thigh. "I was gone for a lot of years, but not long enough that I forgot what happened before I left." He unscrewed the cap on the water bottle, took a sip. "And if this town is in your blood and you're a Donovan or an Alexander, the stories reach you, no matter where you are."

"Were the families feuding?" She'd noticed Rogan's clipped responses when she mentioned the Alexander name, but she'd believed it had to do with the power behind the name rather than some type of feud.

"Were they feuding?" Oliver Donovan let out a laugh that filled the room. "When *weren't* they feuding? Pit two men against each other, put them at cross-purposes, throw in a woman, and you've got a war. Or, in this case, a feud that carries from generation to generation, instilling animosity and a desire for vengeance that goes far beyond a jilted lover."

"But Camille's married to an Alexander."

His expression turned cold. "Yeah, she is, and how's that working out for her?"

From the short time Elizabeth had been in Reunion Gap, she'd say Camille's marriage was a disaster. "Point taken. But the rest? The reason behind the feud? I have no idea what happened or why."

"Of course you don't, because you don't know the history of our town." He saluted her with his water bottle, took a long drink. "Maybe if you're here long enough, someone will tell you." He eyed her. "But it's not going to be me. I'm more interested in how you've gathered so much knowledge in such a short time. I don't think it's Rogan, and Rose gets her facts confused, so consider the source. Jennifer Merrick has her own issues and she's not going to give up big secrets, if she knows any. Plus, she's still considered an outsider, so she wouldn't have all the facts." Those blue eyes turned to steel, the voice soft as it bordered on a warning, "Or maybe it isn't any of them. Maybe it's something else altogether that I haven't considered yet. But I will, no worries there. I'm very good at solving puzzles and you, Elizabeth Hastings, are a very intriguing puzzle."

That last comment unsettled her, though she kept her composure until she was back in her SUV, punching out Uncle Everett's phone number. Oliver Donovan was no fool. She'd have to be more careful around the man, and she'd have to be careful around Rogan, too. But how was she supposed to do that when she and Rogan were venturing into a new stage of getting to know each other? It was hard enough to filter her past so she could be honest with him without divulging her father's identity. If only she didn't have to hopscotch around her choice of words and what she shared. And why did Uncle Everett have to be so darn thorough about the residents of this town? Maybe his investigator should have done more of a surface inquiry, but with a person from the town spilling information, she guessed some secrets were bound to land in her uncle's file.

He answered on the third ring. "Elizabeth? Hello, dear. How's life in Reunion Gap?"

"Until ten minutes ago, I would have said excellent." She let out a long sigh, fished her sunglasses from her handbag.

"Oh? What happened?"

"It seems that investigator of yours was much too thorough, and now, Oliver Donovan is wondering how I could know about details that aren't shared with outsiders."

"Hmm."

"And speaking of investigators, did you send your guy here?"

"No. Why do you ask?"

"Because there's some investigator staying at the inn. Isn't your guy named Lester something?"

"Conroy, my dear. Lester Conroy. Texan, born and bred, lives in New York state now. You'll know him if you see him." He chuckled. "The Stetson and the cowboy boots will be a sure giveaway, even before he opens his mouth."

"I hope this isn't your guy." She took a deep breath, tried to calm the agitation swirling through her. "I can't have this blow up in my face. It's too important." *Rogan is too important.*

"Relax, Elizabeth. The man's probably just the curious sort."

"Actually, I told him *I* was the curious one and that's why I knew so much. What do you think he'd say if he knew I had cheat cards on quite a few of the residents, *including him*?"

"I'd say you have to make sure he doesn't find out." Pause. "Nobody can find out who you are, especially the Donovans."

He had no idea how true those words were. "I agree." She glanced across the street and spotted Oliver Donovan leaning against the railing of his shop, arms crossed over his chest, gaze trained on her. He knew she was hiding something and that look said he intended to find out what it was.

TATE ALEXANDER WAS BACK in town.

News of his father's stroke spread through town in waves. The first recounted Harrison Alexander in a heated phone conversation with an unidentified person, according to the household staff. The yelling could be heard from the man's study, bouncing off the walls, and landing in the servants' quarters in an unintelligible rumble. No one had come forth to claim a presence on the other end of the line. There was speculation, though, none of it good.

Bet it was one of his mistresses. Maybe mistress number one found out about mistress number two.

Could have been a deal gone bad, or not the way Harrison expected.

Had to do with money and power, no question. Somebody was getting squeezed, and maybe this time that somebody was Harrison.

Or, and this was the most speculated, *It was his son, Tate.*

Hence came the second wave of information that rolled through town.

Tate Alexander is back in town!

Goodness gracious, it's a miracle…

Six long years away…

Will he stay?

Will he make Reunion Gap his home again?

Rogan had heard the rumors, but he'd tried to ignore most of them. He didn't want to think about Tate, the one Alexander he could tolerate until the guy betrayed him. And his father? Was there even a speck of decency in the man? Doubtful. He pushed aside thoughts of the Alexanders and went back to installing a light fixture, but damn if Elizabeth didn't creep into his brain. This was getting ridiculous. The woman had taken up residence in his head, and if he were honest, he'd admit she'd set up house in his heart, too. In less than six hours they'd get together, talk about likes and dislikes, hopes and disappointments. He sighed, muttered a curse under his breath. *They'd share.*

That word was as unfamiliar as its meaning, but it was necessary in any long-term relationship. They both knew it, had agreed to it, though he'd felt like he was going to puke when he suggested it, and she looked like she might join him. Slow and steady so he didn't scare her or himself.

He hadn't wanted to share with anyone in a long time.

But Elizabeth was different.

Or maybe *she* made him different.

The door to his storefront accounting office opened and Rogan glanced up at the visitor. A man, tall, mid-thirties, dark hair, nice suit. Tate Alexander.

"Hello, Rogan."

Tate Alexander moved toward him with the casual grace that comes with being born into money, and lots of it. The guy had never seemed interested in the money, had almost acted apologetic when a stranger found out he was an Alexander. But there was no getting around the name or the power it wielded. Rogan tossed his pencil on the desk, crossed his arms over his chest. "I heard you were back. Sorry about your father."

"Thanks." He pointed to one of the chairs across from Rogan. "Mind if I sit?"

"Sure." Why was he here? It better not have to do with—

"I did not touch Marybeth." Those silver eyes burned into him. "I wouldn't do that to you."

And there it was. "Are we really going to bring that up after all these years?" The guy hadn't exactly been Rogan's friend, but he hadn't been his enemy either. If circumstances were different and the family patriarchs hadn't despised one another and insisted the feud continue, Tate and Rogan might have found common ground and a friendship buried in there somewhere. But any possibility of that died when Rogan's girlfriend claimed Tate stole a bottle of his father's bourbon and got her drunk. Marybeth said she didn't remember anything else, but when half-naked pictures of her started floating around school two days later, Tate Alexander got the blame and a black eye from Rogan.

Marybeth never filed any formal charges because she was, after all, involved in underage drinking. Plus, it was her word against Tate's. No surprise that the Alexander family once again walked away from a potential scandal. Odd thing was, Tate admitted to the drinking, but he swore on his great-grandfather's 1963 Cadillac that he delivered Marybeth Caruthers home that night, fully clothed and untouched at 11:59 p.m. Rogan never had understood what the two of them were doing together and Tate wouldn't say anything other than *trying to find out the truth about Marybeth Caruthers*, whatever that meant.

Tate cleared his throat. "If we're going to be living in the same town again, I think we have to talk about it since we never dealt with it the first time."

Rogan picked up his pencil, fiddled with it. Why was it the guy could irritate the crap out of him just by opening his mouth? "There's nothing to talk about. Whether you did or didn't undress my old girlfriend and take half-nude photos of her isn't the point." He stared Tate down, didn't try to hide the animosity in his voice. "You know, I always wondered how Marybeth could afford an Ivy League education when her mother worked as a cook at the school and her father was a postman." He rubbed his jaw, waited for Tate to respond. Nothing but a clenched fist and a twitch on the right side of his jaw. "Yeah, I figured your family fixed things, nice and neat, with college tuition included." He jabbed the tip of his pencil into a note pad. "And *that's* the point."

"I didn't touch her and I didn't take those damn pictures."

"Right."

"I was as pissed off about the whole deal as you were. You think I liked having the town believe I undressed her, took pictures, and *circulated* them? That is sick on so many levels, almost as sick as having my old man pay her off. I was innocent and I wasn't allowed to prove it." The hollowness in his words said he'd suffered as much as Rogan, maybe more. "My father put a lid on it, told me we were never to discuss the 'unfortunate' incident again, and if I did, he'd yank my college tuition. Imagine your father not *caring* if you were guilty or innocent of hurting someone, a woman no less."

Rogan shifted in his chair, studied the paperwork on his desk. The whole town knew what a ruthless bastard Harrison Alexander was, how he treated his family like possessions and sometimes like pawns in his games of manipulation and control. "I think we should bury this topic."

Tate's lips pulled into a thin line. "Not until we've cleared the air."

"It's clear as mud, but if we keep digging we might have to ask ourselves who tried to set you up and why? And what part

Marybeth played in all of this. Since word has it you're hanging around a while, we need to try and get along. Speaking of, *why are you* hanging around?"

The bitterness in Tate's voice stretched across the desk. "Duty, same as you. When I heard the old man had a stroke, I knew I had to come back. I couldn't dump this situation on Neal or Meredith. Good thing I didn't wait for them, because they're both MIA. I can't blame them, though; the old man was nothing but miserable and judgmental with them."

"So, how long will you stay?"

Tate shrugged. "No idea. When I got here, the company lawyer told me the board voted me in to run the place while my father was incapacitated." He blew out a breath that sounded an awful lot like frustration. "As if I don't have a job and a life in Chicago. I thought about telling them all to go screw themselves, but I couldn't do it. Anyway, maybe some good will come of this."

"How so?"

He shrugged again, looked Rogan square in the eye. "I'll have direct access to company files. That means I can poke around and make sure everything's on the up and up."

That sounded like Tate suspected his father might be involved in underhanded dealings. "What will you do if you find out everything isn't on the up and up?" That was the real question with a multitude of possibilities.

"Then it's going to get tricky." He hesitated, said in a quiet voice, "And I'll have some tough choices to make."

"Lucky you."

"Right. Lucky me."

"Thanks for letting me know you're back in town."

Tate stood. "What's that crazy sister of yours up to these days? Still fighting her causes?"

Had his expression softened just now? Rogan pushed back his

chair, eyed the man who women had once called "irresistible." Had his little sister thought this guy was irresistible, too? Damn well better not have. "Charlotte's in Nashville."

"I see."

Was that disappointment in his voice? He wasn't about to tell the guy she'd be home soon. Let Tate Alexander think Charlotte intended to remain well out of reach—hundreds of miles away, safe, exactly where she belonged.

9

Rogan left the doors to the building open so he could work in the cool night air. He'd grown used to air-conditioning when he lived in California, and it had been an adjustment to return to an area that didn't consider it essential. He'd given up a lot of *essentials*: a penthouse view, a hot tub, box seats at the Lakers games. As the months passed, their absence bothered him less.

Tonight, he wasn't thinking about essentials or air-conditioning. All he wanted to do was finish the plans for the next phase of this project so he could get Oliver's opinion. And then he'd lock up and head over to The Oak Table where he planned to meet Elizabeth for drinks. He'd seen her the last two nights, shared a mushroom and spinach pizza with her at the local Italian restaurant, walked around town and ended up at the ice cream shop for homemade salted caramel ice cream. This Sunday, his mother had invited her for baked halibut, asparagus, and twice-baked potatoes.

They'd done a hell of a lot of talking, too, and it hadn't been difficult or painful. For a guy who liked to keep his thoughts to himself, he'd been pretty open about sharing them. Elizabeth made it easy. Maybe because she listened, or maybe because she really seemed to care about what he had to say. Or, maybe it had more to do with the whole mutual sharing, mutual trust thing they were working on. Yeah, he'd bet that last one had a lot to do with it, but the others were important, too. He checked his watch, flipped through the music on his phone until he found AC/DC's "Dirty Deeds," and hummed along as he worked.

"Well, if it isn't the long-lost Rogan Donovan."

He swung around, came face-to-face with his old Thursday-night partner. "Alyssa?"

Her red lips pulled into a wide smile. "Surprise." She closed the distance between them, flung her arms around his neck, and planted a soft kiss on his lips. "I've missed you."

Rogan stood, eased her away and stepped back. "What…what are you doing here?"

Those brown eyes glittered. "I've missed you, silly. You've never skipped a Thursday, except for the time you got the stomach flu, but you've cancelled the last three." She tucked a lock of black hair behind her ear, studied him. "That's not like you."

Rogan cleared his throat, avoided her gaze. "I've been busy." How could he tell her Elizabeth Hastings was the reason he cancelled? Women didn't like hearing that another woman had bumped them off the playing field, even when they'd insisted the relationship they shared with you was free and easy. No strings. Right. It sure didn't sound like Alyssa was no-strings right now. As a matter of fact, it sounded as if she had a noose and it was headed for his neck.

"Busy?" She inched toward him, pressed her toned body against his. "Too busy for some fun?" Alyssa trailed her tongue along the left side of his neck, sucked the tender flesh. "Delicious," she murmured.

"Alyssa." Rogan glanced at his watch, realized he should

have left to meet Elizabeth ten minutes ago. "Alyssa," he said again, trying to disengage himself from her grasp. "This really isn't a good time." He might as well have been talking to the chair because she ignored him, continued her assault on his neck.

"I've always wondered about this place…all these months and you've never invited me here." More kissing, more sucking. "Why don't we try out this table? It will give you something to think about while we're apart." She eased back, undid the strings of her red sundress, and let it fall in a heap at her sandaled feet. Alyssa stood in front of him, naked except for a scrap of black thong. Tanned, beautiful, sexy as hell.

But she wasn't Elizabeth.

A month ago, casual sex with Alyssa was enough.

Not now, not since Elizabeth.

Rogan knelt to retrieve the sundress, slid it up her thighs, over her waist, and had begun tying the straps when he glanced up and found Elizabeth standing just inside the room, shock and disbelief etched on her face. Before he could speak, she turned and ran. "Elizabeth! Wait!" He started to go after her, but four steps later, fingernails dug into his skin, stopped him.

"Who was that?" When he didn't answer, those dark eyes narrowed and Alyssa spat out, "Who was that, Rogan? Is she my replacement?"

A replacement? Elizabeth didn't replace women like Alyssa. Elizabeth was unique, special, and she did not deserve to witness what she'd just seen. Rogan stared at his former Thursday-night hookup, wondered how he'd never seen the possessiveness before. Had he not been looking or had he believed what she'd said about no strings because that's what *he* wanted? "We had fun, Alyssa, and I enjoyed spending time with you, but I never promised you more than that."

She planted her hands on her hips, stuck her chin up. "Fun?

Oh, we had fun, Rogan Donovan, and don't you dare tell me you didn't enjoy it because I know you did."

He nodded. No sense denying the woman had a bag of sexual tricks and knew how to use it. "I'm not denying it."

Her red lips quivered. "Then why won't you give me a chance to be more to you?" Her voice wobbled, split open. "I could be more…I *want* to be more."

"I'm sorry, but it's not going to happen." He squeezed her hand, said in a gentle voice, "Find somebody who'll treat you the way you deserve. Don't settle for less."

She blinked hard, sniffed. "I saw the way you looked at her. Like your whole world rested in her hands. You never looked at me like that, Rogan, not even in my dreams."

It took another fifteen minutes and a good cry before Alyssa was ready to head home. When she left, Rogan hopped in his car and headed to the Peace & Harmony Inn. He had to talk to Elizabeth, explain that what she saw wasn't what it looked like. Well, not exactly. She'd probably want to know about Alyssa—who wouldn't ask questions about a naked woman standing a foot away from the man who was supposed to be falling for her?

What a mess!

When he arrived at the inn he parked the car, hopped out and headed up the porch steps. Jennifer Merrick opened the front door before he had a chance to ring the bell, and from the look on her face, she already knew about the activities at the shop tonight. "Where is she?" No need to say her name because they both knew he meant Elizabeth.

"I'm not sure she wants to see you right now."

The tightness in the woman's voice told him she'd known her share of heartache, probably at the hands of a man. Still, he had to make things right with Elizabeth. Somehow. "I need to see her. Please?"

"Don't hurt her, Rogan. If you can't be honest with her, leave her alone." When he nodded, she stepped aside and motioned toward the stairs. "It's the third room on the right."

He took off toward the stairs, climbed them two at a time, and took a deep breath once he reached her door. Was she crying? Rogan placed his ear against the door, listened. Damn, but she *was* crying. He cursed himself for hurting her and vowed to heal that hurt. Then he knocked and waited.

"Yes?"

Rogan opened the door, stepped inside. Elizabeth had her head buried in her hands, the muffled sobs piercing his heart. He moved toward her, sank onto the bed next to her. "Elizabeth?"

She lifted her head, her face tear-stained and swollen, eyes streaked with mascara. "What are you doing here?" And then, "Go away."

"I need to talk to you." He paused, swallowed, tried again. "About what you saw at the shop."

Those amber eyes burned right through him. "What I saw at the shop? The actions were pretty self-explanatory."

Rogan clasped her hand, held it. "But that's just it. They weren't self-explanatory." If she would only give him a chance to explain, he could make this right. "Nothing was going to happen between me and Alyssa."

She raised an eyebrow. "Then someone should have told her."

He nodded, held her hand tighter. "I know. There's a fine line between hurting a person's feelings and getting roped into something you don't want to do." Until Elizabeth walked into his life, he'd been better than okay with the arrangement he and Alyssa had. No strings, no expectations. That all changed when he met Elizabeth. With her he *wanted* a lot more than a few laughs and a good time.

The frown she gave him said she wasn't interested in anything but what she saw. "Do not even try to make me believe you weren't interested in her. What man wouldn't want to be with someone like that?"

Rogan met her gaze, held it, and said in a quiet voice, "This man."

Fresh tears trickled down her cheeks, landed on her blouse. "Don't."

"Don't what? Admit the truth?" He leaned closer, brushed a tear from her cheek. "I'm sorry I hurt you, but I promise whatever happened between me and Alyssa was over the first time I saw you."

She pulled away, stared at him. "I'm not good at games, Rogan. I don't understand them and I don't play them."

"No games. Just you and me." She appeared so damn vulnerable right now, nothing like the way he was used to seeing her: composed, in control. He wanted to protect her, wanted to dry the tears and promise he'd never be the cause of them again. But that would be a lie because people who cared about each other still caused hurt, even if they didn't intend it. "I'm sorry I hurt you." Rogan brushed another tear from her cheek. "I can't promise I'll never hurt you again because that would be a lie, and I won't lie to you. But what I will do…what I *want* to do, is try very hard not to hurt you." He cupped her chin, lost himself in those amber eyes, and murmured, "I care about you, Elizabeth. A lot."

The kiss came next, a feather-light touch of lips against lips, and then, "I care about you, too." A soft sigh. "Too much, I think."

Her words made Rogan's chest ache, gave him hope. He kissed her again, murmured, "There will never be too much for us." Another kiss, a stroke of her jaw. "Only not enough."

She pulled away, her eyes bright, lips parted. "Don't hurt me, Rogan."

"Never."

There was no talking after that as they touched and kissed,

their soft sighs and low moans cocooning them in a world where no one else existed. Had he ever felt this close to a woman—in bed, fully clothed? No, he sure as hell hadn't. But Elizabeth was different. Enjoying her body wouldn't be enough. He wanted all of her—body, heart, and soul.

Would she give them to him?

She squirmed beneath him, placed his hand on her breast, a sign he recognized as "touch me."

How could he refuse?

Rogan unbuttoned the first button of Elizabeth's blouse, then the second, the third… When she moaned, he trailed his tongue along the rim of her lacy pink bra, tasted the tender flesh. Another moan escaped her lips, this one louder, more urgent. *That* he recognized as need *and* want. If he didn't stop now, he wouldn't stop until they were undressed and he was deep inside her. Forget the undressed part. They could do that the second time.

But there wasn't going to be a first or second time until he was certain Elizabeth wanted this, too, and not as an emotional reaction to tonight, but as the beginning of a future—their future. He opened his mouth to speak, hesitated. Hadn't he said they should get to know one another before they slept together? Yes, that idiot who said those words had really been him. He tried to ignore the erection throbbing between them, and said, "Maybe we should stop."

"Stop?" Her brows pinched together. "You want to stop?"

Was she mad? Or was that confusion? Disappointment? Hurt? Damn, but he couldn't tell. "Of course, I don't *want* to stop. No man with half an ounce of testosterone would want to stop, but I don't want to screw things up between us by getting physical with you too soon."

"Getting physical?" Her lips twitched. "Is this an exercise class?"

Was she making fun of him? He found nothing humorous in

the situation, or in her comments. "I'm trying to respect you, Elizabeth, so cut me some slack, okay? I usually don't have to consider so many situations because I'm not looking for long-term."

Her expression softened, her voice fell out in a whisper, "Thank you for your honesty. And for caring about me." She eased a hand to the opening of his shirt, unbuttoned the top button. "You're a good person, Rogan. I hope I never disappoint you."

"How could you ever disappoint me?"

She shrugged, looked away for a second, and he thought the tears were about to start again. "I know we haven't known each other long, but I feel safe with you, and I trust you. I've only been able to say that to a few people in my whole life." She worked up a smile, stroked his cheek. "I want to be with you, Rogan. Will you stay tonight?"

He nodded. "Of course." His heart burst with happiness, but his crotch wanted clarification. What exactly did she mean by asking him to stay the night? Did she mean naked and making love, or did she mean clothed and cuddling? In the grand scheme of their future, did it really matter? Could he not give up one night of pleasure with her, or two, or ten, if it meant forging a deeper bond?

"I just have one more request. If you're agreeable…" She eased his shirt open, ran her hands down his chest.

"Yes?" What else could she possibly want? Sleep naked but don't make love? Torture. Touch each other, but don't make love? Again, more torture. "What is it?"

A smile inched over her face. "Make love to me?"

Rogan let out a sigh, said in his most serious voice, "Absolutely. I will do my best not to disappoint."

And he did exactly that.

Three times.

And if the moans of pleasure and whimpers of delight were any indication, Elizabeth was not disappointed.

~

"So, you and Rogan Donovan, huh?"

Elizabeth poured a cup of coffee, glad for the extra few seconds to gather her thoughts. Jennifer had let Rogan in last night, so she knew he'd been here, but did she know he stayed? He'd started to leave around 1:30 a.m., but one good-night kiss turned into shedding his clothes and crawling back into bed to make love—again. When she woke a few hours later, he was gone, a note resting on his pillow. *See you tonight, R.*

"Look, if you don't want to talk about it, I understand. He's a good guy, and he deserves some happiness." Jennifer paused. "It's just that nobody's been able to snag him, and trust me, women have tried."

Elizabeth turned, faced Jennifer and said in a quiet voice, "I guess we'll see where this goes." Rogan had admitted his inability to trust and get close to another woman after his fiancée broke things off, but he'd also told her he hadn't wanted to, until he met her. Panic started in her belly, spread to her heart, her lungs, her brain. He did mean what he said, didn't he? He wouldn't lie to her.

Would he?

Just because she'd caught a half-naked woman at JD Manufacturing last night in what looked like a very compromising situation didn't mean he'd been about to accept her invitation. He'd said he wasn't interested in the woman, hadn't been interested since he met Elizabeth. And she believed him.

Didn't she?

"I don't mean to upset you." Jennifer shook her head, set a yogurt parfait mixed with strawberries, blueberries, and walnuts in front of Elizabeth. "Really, I'm sorry I said anything. Forget about it, okay?"

Why had her voice cracked just now, and why did she look like she might cry? "Jennifer? Are you okay? Does this have anything to do with the investigator?"

Jennifer bit her bottom lip, swallowed. "How do you know about him?"

"Oliver told me."

"Ugh. Why can't that man mind his own business?" A groan of disgust and annoyance slipped out. "Why does he have to nose around and comment like he knows what's going on? He doesn't know." Her voice cracked, her shoulders shook. "He doesn't know *anything*."

Elizabeth stood, moved toward the woman she'd come to consider a friend. "I'm sorry; I didn't mean to upset you." She placed a hand on Jennifer's arm, squeezed. "Have you really not figured out why Oliver gets involved with anything that has to do with you and Hope?"

"Because he's a self-righteous pain in the butt who loves to offer opinions on how we can all improve our lives by opening our hearts to positive thoughts and forgiveness." She mumbled something under her breath. "I am so tired of that man and I'm tempted to tell him to shove his good-thoughts crap and leave me alone." Her blue eyes glistened with tears. "But how can I do that to Hope? I can't take away the one person aside from me she trusts."

"Oh, Jennifer, don't you see why he acts the way he does? I'm terrible at this stuff, and it's obvious to me. Do you really not know?"

"I told you why he does it. He thinks he's better than people like me who get mad, carry grudges, and live with anger. You'd think he was the Dalai Lama, walking the earth, scattering his good intentions on us mortals."

"I don't think Oliver's trying to make you or anybody else feel inferior to him. Jennifer, he cares about you."

"Of course he cares." She frowned, swiped at a tear. "I told you, he thinks he's the Dalai Lama."

"No, that's not what I'm talking about. Oliver cares about you, as in a man-woman relationship."

"Oliver? Interested in *me*?" Those eyes widened, the lips pulled into a straight line. "That is absolutely the craziest idea I've ever heard."

Elizabeth shrugged. "Nobody said relationships don't have crazy moments. I think you should talk to him, and while you're at it, tell him about this investigator. He seemed very concerned when he asked me about it. If there's an issue, my guess is he'll be able to help you with it."

Jennifer hesitated as if considering the wisdom of a face-to-face conversation with Oliver Donovan. But when she spoke, there was a sliver of hope in her words. "Maybe he *can* help."

OLIVER GRABBED a ginger ale and a Tom Petty and the Heartbreakers CD and headed for the back porch with Maybelline. Nothing better than listening to classic rock 'n' roll and counting stars with your best four-legged girl. He was already thinking about it when he heard a knock at the front door that sent Maybelline into a barking frenzy and a beeline toward the sound. Some people really did not understand the meaning of *closed*. The knocking continued, more forceful than before. That escalated the barks, turned them into high-pitched yelps. He set down the drink and the CD and made his way to the front door. "Maybelline, leave it." The barking stopped, and she sat, eyeing him for a good-girl treat. Talk about Pavlov's dog… Oliver held up a hand.

"Stay." Then he opened the door and came face-to-face with the last person he expected to find.

Jennifer Merrick.

"Jennifer?" Something must be very wrong for her to come here. "What's wrong? Is Hope okay?"

"Yes, she's fine." She cleared her throat. "May I come in?"

"Sure." He stepped aside, took in the faint tear streaks on her cheeks, the swollen nose. Something was definitely wrong. Did it have to do with the investigator who'd come poking around?

"So, this is Maybelline," she said, smiling at his best friend. "Hope's told me all about her."

"That's her all right. Most spoiled French bull dog on this planet." He could try to sound gruff and annoyed, but who was he kidding? This dog was family and she knew it.

Jennifer leaned down, ran both hands along her back in a way that made Maybelline wiggle and let out a satisfied snort. "She's darling."

"Yeah, and she knows it, too. I was just heading out back to enjoy the night with Tom Petty. Why don't you join me?" When she nodded, he grabbed his drink and the CD. "Follow me. Can I get you something? I've got iced tea, ginger ale…"

"I'll have what you're having."

"Ginger ale it is." He made his way to the mini fridge he kept in the back room and grabbed a can of ginger ale. "Here you go," he said, handing it to her.

"Thank you."

There was an almost smile on her lips and her voice held a note of something close to gratitude. What the hell was going on? Jennifer Merrick had never looked at him with gratitude and he'd bet his last record she'd never said a kind word about him. "Hold on a sec." Oliver popped in the CD, turned it down to an after-dark-acceptable level and held the screen door to the back porch open to let her pass. "I'm not particular about my chairs, so pick whichever one you want." That was a bold-faced lie. His chair was the rocker closest to the door with the padded cushion that molded to his butt from long hours sitting on the damn thing. Of course, that was the one she picked, and Maybelline plopped right at her feet. *Traitor.*

He sank into the other rocker, took a drink, and turned to her. The porch lights illuminated her profile: the straight nose, the pinched lips, the slender neck. And those crazy ball earrings she always wore. What was the story behind them? There had to be one because he'd never seen a woman with such an affinity for glass ball earrings—always the same ones: red with gold swirls.

She sipped her ginger ale, clutched the can against her middle, and stared into the gray darkness. "You must be wondering why I'm here." A blink, then another, before her voice cracked and snippets of pain slipped out. "I don't know what to do, and while I hate to admit it, you might be the only person in this town who'll listen without judging."

Was that a compliment? A grudging one, no doubt, but it sure sounded like one. "Thank you, I think."

Those pinched lips pulled into a faint smile. "It *is* a compliment."

Joy shot through him, and he told himself it had to do with Tom Petty's "Free Fallin'," but who was he kidding? A compliment from Jennifer Merrick was better than a reunion tour with his old band. "Why don't you tell me what's going on?" She opened her mouth to speak, closed it. After three attempts, Oliver decided to take a chance on the reason behind her hesitancy. "Does any of this have to do with that cowboy investigator who's been snooping around?"

She shot him a glance, eyes wide, fear and pain stretching across her face. "Yes," she whispered.

"Okay, why don't you tell me what happened that would send him here?" He didn't miss the flinch or the way she gripped the can, like it was her last lifeline before she went under. "I can't help if I don't know what's going on." Oliver gentled his voice. "I want to help you, Jen."

"It's about my mother." She held his gaze as the tears streamed down her cheeks, her voice a mix of pain and regret. "Ten years ago, I fell for a man I thought could give me the world. He promised to show me Australia, Italy, Iceland, Spain. He told me he loved me." She swiped at her cheeks. "My parents didn't approve. They said any man who truly cared about a woman wouldn't ask her for money, or a place to stay…or to take out a loan for him. Of course, I didn't listen to them. My brother died in a car accident when he was a teenager, and I always felt like a big piece of my parents died then, too. It wasn't that they ignored me, but their grief was so heavy, they couldn't get past it. They tried so hard to protect me from getting hurt that they smothered me, or at least I thought they did." She shrugged, brushed her hair from her forehead. "Now that I have Hope, I can see how parents would do anything to protect their child. But, I didn't see it at the time."

He'd always wondered about the family Jennifer never talked about, and he'd spent quite a bit of time thinking about Hope's father, too. "So, what happened?"

"What didn't happen? The guy I was with said we should leave Magdalena and make a life together. I didn't know he meant move from place to place like nomads, running up credit card debt, and taking out loans to do it." Her voice wobbled, fell flat. "And steal from my own mother. Yes, I *stole* from her, Oliver, and I didn't think twice about it. What kind of daughter does such a thing?"

"A desperate one who's lost her way," he said in a quiet voice.

"A worthless one who doesn't deserve her parents' love or forgiveness."

Oliver set his ginger ale down, reached across the small table and clasped her forearm. "Don't say that, Jen. It's not true. You made mistakes. Who hasn't? That's called living. I can see you regret them, but if you keep beating yourself up for the past, you'll never be able to move forward." He gentled his voice. "My guess is your mother sent the investigator to find you." When she didn't respond, he prodded, "Am I close?"

A nod, then another. "Why would she want to have anything to do with me after how I treated her? Who does that to their family?" She sniffed. "The man I ran off with left me the second he learned I was pregnant. Too real for him, he said, and besides, how could I travel to all the places we talked about if we had a child? I was never part of his long-term plan. I realized that when he told me if I wanted to get rid of the baby, he'd hang around."

"Jerk." Oliver wasn't a violent man, but if the guy were standing in front of him right now, he'd slug him in the gut.

"Yes, he was, but I wasn't much better. When I left Magdalena, I just disappeared, leaving nothing behind but a note telling them how much I didn't need them in my life because I'd found someone to love and protect me." She let out a harsh laugh. "Imagine that? The guy who wanted me to kill our baby would be my life partner? Hardly."

No wonder Jennifer had erected a wall to keep her emotions in and keep everyone else who might hurt her, out. He understood what he'd long suspected. Jennifer Merrick was damaged and hurting, and it had all happened at the hands of a man she trusted. "Do you want to reconnect with your mother?" Oliver paused. "And what about your father?"

Fresh tears spilled down her cheeks, slid to her chin and onto her shirt. "He's dead. One night, I was feeling really down, questioning my life and all the past mistakes I'd made. I decided to do a computer search of the town where I grew up, and that's when my father's obituary popped up. Can you imagine what *that* felt like?"

Oliver shook his head. "No, I can't. I'm so sorry."

"I was so busy blaming them and everyone else for my unhappiness that I never thought about something happening to one of them. You think you have forever to settle things, but you don't, do you?" Her voice drifted off, grew softer. "Once the opportunity is gone, it's done. No going back. My father died before I ever had a chance to talk to him again. And my mother? She was left all alone to deal with her grief. I could have been there to help." She paused, reworked the sentence. "I *should* have been there to help."

"That's a lot of guilt to carry on such small shoulders." Oliver eased his hand from her arm, settled back in his chair. "If you want to fix things between you and your mother, it's not too late. It's never too late, Jen. She wouldn't be contacting you if she didn't harbor her own share of regrets. But if you're going to attempt to fix things, you've got to open up and be honest with her about everything: your life then and now, your expectations, your regrets, and your wishes for the future." He worked up a smile. "And don't forget to tell her about the shining star in your universe. Imagine how she'd feel to know she's a grandmother."

Jennifer bit her bottom lip. "Hope isn't like other children. What if my mother can't accept her?"

Now she was annoying him. "Hope might not be like other children, but so what? Maybe it's our job to try and understand *her* world. She's intelligent and creative, and a stickler for details. Ever notice how she can alphabetize every appliance that goes in a kitchen? And count the number of petals on a rose without picking it apart?" He laughed, grabbed his drink and took a swig. "I can't do that and I'm a hell of a lot older than she is." Oliver cleared his throat, said, "I meant, I'm a lot older than she is. Sorry about the cuss word."

"I'm not afraid of a cuss word now and again." Jennifer sipped her drink, slid her gaze to him. "And you're not that old."

Okay, now they were getting into uncomfortable territory with talk about him, cussing, and his age. Since when had Jennifer Merrick been okay with *any* of that? He had to steer the conversation back to her and whatever heartache she carried around that caused her such pain. "Let's not get sidetracked. If you want to talk to your mother, I can help make that happen. If you don't want to talk to her, I'll support that decision, too. The last one wouldn't be my choice, but it's not up to me. Either way, you've got to start with an open mind, and an open heart." He pinned her with a no-nonsense look. "But before you can do anything, you've got to forgive yourself."

"Oliver?"

Her soft voice slipped over him, warmed him. "Yes?"

"Thank you." For the first time all night, she offered up a real smile. "I knew you could help."

It wasn't until later that night, as he lay awake in bed, Maybelline snoring beside him, that he replayed each word he and Jen had spoken. Why had he been so eager to help?

Was it because of Hope?

Or had he been trying to show Jen that he really was a decent guy who knew how to solve problems and save damsels in distress when required?

Of course, the last possibility, and the least appealing, was most likely the truth: he had a thing for Jen Merrick and he'd do just about anything for her.

10

Tate slipped into the private room at Reunion Gap Memorial Hospital, stood at the foot of the bed. His father's head lay against the pillow, tilted to the right, a tiny bit of drool hanging from his slack lips. The paleness of his face and arms against the starkness of the hospital sheets unsettled Tate. He couldn't remember a time when his father hadn't been a towering force—tanned, broad, in command...

The hospital called earlier, said they'd noticed some irregularities with his heart and wanted to run tests. Irregularities with the old man's heart? Huh, guess that meant he actually had one. His sister said she'd come if he needed her, but he could read between the lines: *Please don't make me come home.* The old man had ignored Meredith most of her life, treating her as though her opinions didn't matter, and when she'd inquired about joining the company, he'd told her there were no openings. Who said that to their only daughter? No, he wouldn't ask his sister to come home. In fact, he hoped she stayed far away from Reunion Gap and their father's poisonous existence.

As for his brother, if Neal's last phone call could be trusted, he'd be on a plane to Reunion Gap in five days. Why five, Tate wondered, and had been tempted to ask. But what was the point? Whether it was five or fifty-five, his little brother would show up when he was ready, and Tate bet it would be a lot longer than five days.

See what you've done to this family? You've destroyed it, left us with scars so deep we'll never be normal.

Tate moved to the side of the bed, settled his gaze on his father's shallow breaths. How had the man gone from big and in charge to small and feeble? The doctors hadn't said much about his recovery, as in when or to what extent, and Tate hadn't asked. Whether the man could mouth two words or recite a whole book, he was still a bastard.

Why hadn't God taken his father and spared his mother six years ago? She would have been able to enjoy life, her family, and one day, her grandkids. Why did she have to slip away in her sleep and leave them all alone? If He'd taken their old man instead, maybe Tate never would have left Reunion Gap. Maybe he'd have realized that sometimes everything you need is right in front of you, if you stop to look. Like the woman he'd never been able to forget.

The soft moan startled him, made him zero in on the pale face above the sheet. Another moan, followed by a sigh. Tate waited for more, a blink of an eye, a gesture of a hand, even a movement of a finger, but there was nothing. Typical. Harrison Alexander did nothing on anyone else's schedule and fought for control, even now.

The idea that his father could not give up the control he'd so carefully orchestrated for years angered Tate, made him want to lash out. He opened his mouth to speak, closed it. Whether his father was awake, asleep, or semiconscious, Tate would not risk giving the old man the satisfaction of seeing him angry. He stared at his father's closed eyes, let the feelings surge through him without uttering a word.

Hey, old man. Did you have a stroke so I'd come home? Figured you'd get me here one way or another, didn't you? Damn you, why couldn't you be a father to your kids? Do you know what you've done? You've taught us not to trust anyone, least of all ourselves. That kills all chances of a real relationship, but you wouldn't know about that, would you? Have you ever cared about anyone or anything but power and money?

I doubt it.

We are screwed up and that's on you.

Why couldn't you let us live our lives, learn our own lessons like normal people? Because we weren't allowed to be normal, were we? No, we had to be perfect because we were Alexanders.

Screw that, old man.

Tate clenched his fists, cursed under his breath.

I'm running the company now and I'm going to figure out what secrets you've been hiding. Every damn one of them, and then I'm going to make things right.

See if you can stop me.

Tate left the hospital a few minutes later and drove back to the house, his mind on the decrepit shell of a man in the hospital bed. Would he recover? If so, to what degree? The doctor in charge said the progress would be slow and would involve various therapies: physical, occupational, speech. Apparently, they didn't know Harrison Alexander was not a patient man, or maybe they did and that's why they said the outcome depended not only on the damage done by the stroke, but the level of commitment and patience involved.

Good luck with the patience part.

He parked the car in the circular drive and hopped out, glancing at the SUV parked several feet ahead of him. Who was it now? Another delivery person, a repairman? Surely not a visitor poking around. Who would visit other than the hired help?

Tate climbed the wide stone steps that led to the brick three-

136

story with pillars. If he hurried, he could fit in a swim before dinner. The water helped clear his head and gain perspective when situations threatened to spin out of control. Like now, with his father and whatever scheming he'd been involved in that had forced him to sell off part of the company. One of the few advantages of growing up in the massive brick house had been the Olympic-size swimming pool with six lanes, a welcome refuge from the old man's demands and expectations. He'd missed that easy access in Chicago, but an athletic club provided a pool without the hassle of a tyrant father.

He opened the front door, called out, "Anybody home?" Not that he expected anyone other than Astrid or one of the other staff to answer, but when they were kids, his sister and brother would charge at him from the other room, thrust themselves at his body, almost knocking him down. The shrieks and laughter would follow, spill into the other rooms until their mother appeared, held a slender finger to her lips in an attempt to silence them. That meant, *Careful, your father's home*. They'd learned about silence and not voicing their thoughts in the presence of Harrison Alexander, a man his little sister called "Daddy Dictator."

"Tate?" Aunt Camille poked her head from the living room, her face lighting up when she spotted him. "Oh, my heavens, it *is* you!" Her small feet *clickety-clack*ed toward him on the designer heels she'd always favored. "It's so good to see you." She flung her tiny body at him, wrapped her arms around his middle. Tate hugged her, laughed at her excitement. "Aunt Camille, it's always good to see you." He smiled down at her, took in the faint crease lines around the eyes and mouth. She'd always said a woman's best fight against aging was laughter, movement, and a good moisturizer. But she hadn't factored the stress involved with a cheating husband. "You look great, not a day older than the last time I saw you."

She raised an arched brow and swatted his arm. "You are such a sweet boy, but that is nothing more than a fib." Those blue eyes sparkled, the smile spread. "I've told enough of my own to know." A soft sigh escaped her lips. "Oh, but I've missed you."

"You, too."

"Six years is much too long to stay away. Don't let it happen again."

He nodded, leaving the reason for his absence hanging between them. Camille knew why he'd left and she knew why he'd come back. "Sometimes our hand is forced. You know that."

"I do. Damn it all, but I do know that." Her eyes grew bright, her voice soft. "Some people do not deserve the oxygen they're breathing."

Did she mean his father or was she talking about her husband? He guessed both.

Seconds later, she clarified. "I won't apologize for not visiting your father at the hospital. I am not a faker."

Tate nodded. "You've never been one to pretend around the truth." Except where her husband was concerned. That was an area that required a vast amount of latitude for interpretation. "So, how's Uncle Carter doing?"

"Living the life, playing doctor, attending conventions—" she offered a stingy smile "—working so hard."

Was that last part intended as sarcasm or was she serious? Hard to tell. Camille and Carter's marriage had been skidding downhill for years. Carter Alexander might be Tate's blood relative, but he'd been closer to Camille. Was it because he couldn't stand his uncle's arrogant, demeaning manner, or because he could relate to the Donovans better than his own family? Or did it have to do with the fact that her niece was Charlotte Donovan? Tate buried the last possibility, settled on the first and second. "I haven't run into him yet."

"Oh, you will." She cocked her head to one side, tapped a forefinger against her chin. "Stop in at the Cherry Top Diner and you might find him salivating after the waitress. You'll recognize her: twenty-two or so, doe-eyed, eager." She paused. "The usual."

Tate cleared his throat, pushed out an apology. "I'm sorry." He wasn't good at emotions that centered on heartache, betrayal, and a bucket load of angst. No thanks. Way too uncomfortable.

She lifted a slender shoulder, sighed. "It's not your fault. Some men are just faithless hound dogs, always sniffing after the next new scent."

Now that was an interesting visual, and in his uncle's case, probably an accurate one. He'd heard similar accusations about his father. Streams of women used to call the house, a few even showed up at his door, but the old man curtailed the personal appearances. He kept the post office busy, too, with perfume-scented letters and packages Tate assumed were from current or former lovers.

How had the old man done it? Had he used the same line every time, or hadn't he needed a line at all? Maybe the rare smiles and good looks had done it for them. Some women were drawn to men who treated them like property. Others cozied up because they believed they could change the man, and all he needed was the right woman to show him love. Right. Nobody could change Harrison Alexander.

Of course, if Tate had to guess, he'd say the women were attracted to the money behind the old man's name and the power that went with it. Sure, why not suck up to wealth and power, see if any would rub off, or at the very least, work on getting a nice piece of jewelry, say a diamond pendant or a pearl necklace? His father's escapades sickened him.

"Tate?" His aunt clasped his arm, said in a soft voice, "Let it go. Your father's never going to change, not until he draws his last breath." She added, "Probably not even then. I'm just glad you're back, even if he's the reason you came."

"Thank you." He smiled down at her. "I thought I'd take a quick swim and then eat around 7:00. Would you like to stay?"

She leaned on tiptoe, planted a kiss on his cheek. "Thank you. I think I will. You are just the sweetest boy in the world. It's a wonder some girl hasn't snapped you up yet." The look she gave him held ten questions in it. "Or has somebody done that?"

He shook his head. "Nope." That was more a matter of opinion. The girl who'd taken up residence in his heart also owned a huge chunk of real estate in his brain. But those admissions were not open for discussion.

"There's someone I want you to meet." Camille clasped his hand and pointed toward the living room. "She's in there." When he stalled, she laughed. "Don't worry; it's not a set-up. She's an artist and I wanted her opinion on a few of your father's paintings. Besides," she leaned close, whispered, "Rogan's already laid claim."

"Rogan?" Last he heard, the guy had sworn off relationships when his fiancée dumped him. Something about not interested in waiting it out while he headed home to settle things for his parents. Talk about not wanting to be inconvenienced. The guy was better off without somebody like that. Would she have wanted to negotiate the number of stretch marks she'd consider permissible in pregnancy? Or maybe pregnancy would have been off the table, or at least, surrogacy would have been the choice. "Where is she?" Tate asked, curious to see the kind of woman Rogan chose to spend his time with and if she'd be long-term.

"This way." Camille motioned for him to follow her.

The second Tate spotted the curvy blonde with the girl-next-door face, he knew Rogan Donovan wasn't giving this one up. Could he blame him? The whiskey-colored eyes, the full lips, the curves…damn, what man wouldn't want a woman like this? But when she spoke, sophistication meshed with gentleness, and when she smiled, well, Tate was surprised Donovan hadn't shoved a ring on her finger yet.

It was coming.

No doubt about it.

Tate smiled, extended a hand. "Tate Alexander. Glad to meet you." She shook his hand, her grip firm, decisive.

"I've heard about you."

He raised a brow. "I'm sure you have." Had her boyfriend filled her in on all the reasons he didn't like Tate? Or had the residents given her the background on the dysfunctional Alexander family: the cruel father, the timid mother, the brow-beaten children? It didn't matter, because people drew their own conclusions about the Alexanders, including him, whether those conclusions were true or not.

And that's why he'd loved Chicago so much. There was no history, nobody to tell him who he was and wasn't, based on his family name.

But now he was back in Reunion Gap, and everybody would have an opinion about his departure *and* his return, even this stranger. He could tell by the look on Elizabeth's face that whatever she'd heard about him had her curious, but she was too polite to ask. His aunt, however, was not the least bit hesitant to enlighten her.

"Tate and Rogan are two of my favorite nephews." She threw an arm around Tate's waist, leaned against him. "Strong, handsome, intelligent, driven—" she paused, smiled up at him "—dedicated, honest, hard-working…"

Tate laughed and glanced at Elizabeth. "Does this sound like a prejudiced opinion? You can't trust an aunt who believes her nephews are perfect. Rogan and I know the real story."

Camille released her hold on him, let out a soft huff. "What do you two know?" She turned to Elizabeth. "I told Tate you and Rogan are seeing each other, and we're all very happy about it.

Well, I can't say *everyone* is happy because I'm sure the females within a hundred-mile radius are shedding tears, but I say too bad for them. They never stood a chance once Elizabeth arrived in Reunion Gap. Oh, I'm sorry dear, am I embarrassing you? Please, don't be embarrassed. Love is a wonderful thing and finding the right person among all the wrong ones?" A long sigh that sifted through her next words, "Well, that is pure magic. When the right one comes along, nothing else matters; not the amount of time you've known each other, the past disappointments, or the future uncertainties. All that matters is being together and staying together. No matter what."

How could she utter those words when she was married to a scumbag like his uncle? Did she really believe what she'd said, or were those feelings for everyone *but* her? Tate darted a glance at Elizabeth, spotted the pink creeping up her neck to her cheeks. Talk about embarrassed *and* humiliated. He was pretty sure she was both, but once Camille started on her happily-ever-after matchmaking spiel, it was hard to stop her. She'd tried it on him a few times and the results had been disastrous.

Except for that one time years ago when she'd attempted to set him up with Charlotte Donovan and he'd no-showed. Yeah, that was not something he cared to think about, but Charlotte would never let him forget about it. Of course, she'd brought it up when he saw her in Chicago, and of course, she'd told him she'd never forgive him for being such a jerk…but she'd forgotten about it for a few hours that night…

"Tate?" Camille had that look on her face that said she was homing in on her next subject, and he was it. "Did you hear what I just said? You look like you're in your own world." She shook her head, narrowed her gaze on him. "I told Elizabeth we've got to find somebody for you next. Rogan is going to settle down; why shouldn't you?"

"Camille." Elizabeth's face had gone from pink to purple. "Rogan and I have only been out a few times."

Tsk-tsk. "Of course, you're only just getting to know one another, but my sources tell me you two have gotten very close lately." The pink lips pulled into a slow smile. "There's nothing like new love—fresh, alive, hopeful. I wouldn't be surprised if you weren't holding a baby this time next—"

"Aunt Camille." Tate burst through his aunt's ramblings before Elizabeth exploded with humiliation.

"What? Marriage doesn't always come before the baby, you know." She eyed him as if to suggest he might consider this route if he were marriage-shy.

"That's not what I'm talking about. Why don't you let Rogan and Elizabeth's relationship develop on its own? That's the best course, don't you think?" He offered her one of the smiles he knew would soften her up, get her to agree with him. That silly smile worked most of the time on most of the women he knew— Charlotte Donovan excluded.

"Perhaps I've been a bit overzealous." Camille clasped Elizabeth's hand. "I think Tate might be right. We should leave you and Rogan alone." She paused, arched a brow. "For now."

FOR THE FIRST time since he'd left California, Rogan's world had started to shine brighter, his hope for a second chance at love and happiness rekindled. He could pretend he didn't know the reason, but that would be a grand lie, and he wasn't into fabrication. The reason for the shift in his universe centered around one woman.

Elizabeth.

No denying that.

He pictured her blonde head on his chest, her arm flung over his belly, the soft sighs of post-pleasure filling the room. They'd spent the last three nights together, with him crawling out of her bed in the early morning hours to make it home in time to shower and head to work. But last night, he hadn't been able to bring himself to leave. Their lovemaking had been so intense, so surreal, he *couldn't* leave her. When he woke this morning to find her next to him, his heart swelled, filled with a joy he'd never known. And when he made love to her minutes later, that joy spread, exploded, and settled between them in what he'd later recognize as true peace.

How could he ever give that up? The answer was clear and simple; he couldn't. Not only that, he wouldn't. For a logical person like himself, falling for a woman this hard and fast was illogical, ill-timed, and certainly ill-advised.

And yet none of it mattered.

He was crazy about Elizabeth Hastings. Damn it, he was half in love with her. Who was he kidding? He was chest-deep in love with her and if this was his second chance, then damn it, he was not going to lose it. Summer would be over soon and with it, her stay in Reunion Gap. The thought of Elizabeth leaving him made his gut churn and his head pound.

What if she didn't have to leave? What if she had a reason to *stay*? Hadn't she told him how much she liked it here, enjoyed spending time with his family? She hadn't met Luke or Charlotte yet, but she would...eventually. Her family was gone, all except an uncle who wasn't really an uncle. Why couldn't she draw in Reunion Gap? Rogan turned back to his paperwork, but it was impossible to concentrate. Elizabeth owned his brain *and* his heart right now, and until he knew exactly where they stood, he doubted he'd get much work done.

Maybe he'd broach the subject tonight. His mother had invited her over for stuffed pork chops, homemade applesauce, parsley-buttered potatoes, and green beans. Was there a peach cobbler tossed in there somewhere? He couldn't remember, but knowing his mother, there'd be way too much food, and even more questions about the future of her son and his new lady.

Rogan spent the next hour thinking about what he'd say to Elizabeth tonight. What if she refused to move to Reunion Gap? What then? He couldn't leave his mother, and he had to see his father's vision through, at least until it was up and running. Elizabeth hadn't asked about investing in the company since the night he'd refused her, but he knew she'd ask again. Anyone who was that impassioned about a project was not about to give up without several more tries. Should he let her invest? Or should he consider a loan? She'd been willing to do both or either one, whatever he wanted. That offer had left him feeling edgy, and he still didn't like it, though he couldn't say why. Maybe because it reminded him of how his father had been taken in by a smooth-talking swindler who offered a deal that was too good to be real, because it wasn't real.

But Elizabeth wasn't Gordon T. Haywood, and she wasn't a swindler or a fake. She was real, and honest, a truly good person.

And he'd fallen in love with her. His gut and his heart told him they belonged together—sharing a house, a life, the Donovan name…

He was still debating what he'd say to Elizabeth this evening when Tate Alexander strolled into his office, tossed a file on his desk. "Ever hear of a guy named Phillip Hayes?"

"Ever hear about pleasantries, like 'hello, how are you?' or 'hey, what's up'?"

Tate grinned, sank into one of the chairs opposite Rogan's desk. "Hello, how are you? Hey, what's up?"

Rogan shook his head, muttered, "Asshole."

The grin spread. "Yup, that's me. Class A asshole, but at least you always know what you're going to get." He pointed to the file on Rogan's desk. "So, have you ever heard of a guy named Phillip Hayes?"

"Hayes?" Rogan rubbed his jaw, opened the file. "Doesn't sound familiar. Why? What's he done?"

"I'm not sure, but I'm going to find out. My father bankrolled the guy around the time the building deal with your dad and Haywood went belly up. There's no documentation or correspondence in the file, not even a business card." He paused, his silver gaze narrowed. "Looks like the company wrote Hayes four checks, $25,000 each."

"Hmm."

"Yeah. Something doesn't feel right."

Rogan scanned the copies of the checks. "Phillip Hayes." He typed the name in his computer, cursed under his breath. "Do you know how many Phillip Hayeses there are?" Another curse, followed by a sigh. "Got any kind of address?"

"Nope. Told you, I've got nothing but those checks. Let me see if I can find out what bank and state the checks are drawn on. That might help us find the guy."

"Why would you want to do that? If he's guilty, he could implicate your father."

Tate's jaw twitched. "That's right, he could."

Rogan closed the file, leaned back in his chair. "You've been gone a long time, maybe too long. Your family doesn't deal in aboveboard and honest. They work side deals and back room handshakes; it's always been that way and you're naive if you think anything's changed."

"It's going to change, trust me on that one. With my old man in the hospital and me at the helm of the company, I've got plenty of time to snoop around. I'm flagging everything that looks questionable, starting with the curiously thin file on Phillip Hayes." He paused, rubbed his jaw. "I *am* going to find the guy. Even if my father regains his speech, he'll never tell me what really happened. But one way or another, I'll get to the bottom of this mess."

Maybe Tate Alexander *could* help. "Thanks." Rogan stood, held out a hand. "I appreciate your help."

"You're welcome." Tate eased out of his chair, shook Rogan's hand. "One of these days, you might just realize I'm not like my father, even if I am an Alexander." Then he flashed a smile and said, "By the way, I met Elizabeth today. Nice girl. Send me an invitation when you set the date."

11

"When are you going to dump his sorry butt?"

Camille pulled a lace handkerchief from her satchel, dabbed her eyes. "It's not that simple, Oliver. You can't just dump the man who's fathered your children and supported you for twenty-nine years."

"Which bothers you more, Cammie? The fact that you'd be dumping the father of your children or losing your meal ticket?" There, he'd said what had been on his mind since the first time he heard his jerk brother-in-law was having an affair too many years ago. His sister liked to compartmentalize her life, but when that life was sinking into a cesspool of lies and dishonesty, with one life jacket remaining, somebody had to call BS on it.

"How can you ask a question like that? Do you think I'd choose money over my children?" Those eyes flashed with the fury he wished she'd show her husband.

"Not money." Oliver paused, reworked his thoughts. "But I do think you like the security, *and* the status of being an Alexander."

"*That* is not true." She huffed her outrage, but there was no oomph in the words.

"Sure it is, but I'm not judging you." He shrugged. "Just

calling what I see. I wish I'd said something the first time you came to me with news that he'd been using his exam table for more than exams."

"Chastity Vanderline. Office secretary." She scrunched her nose. "Perky, plump, and petulant."

When was she going to realize it didn't matter who they were or what they looked like? This was about Carter Alexander, big man on campus with an *M.D.* after his name and an ego larger than the state of California. "He won't stop until he's worked his way through the alphabet, and then he'll start all over again."

His sister's face crumbled right in front of him. "What is wrong with me? Why can't I be enough for him?" Tears drenched her face, her shoulders slumped, her lips quivered. "Why does he always want someone who *isn't* me?"

She asked him this question every time she learned he had a new mistress. And every time, his answer was the same. "This has nothing to do with you, Cammie. It's that bastard you're married to who has the problem. Look at the types of women he picks. Every single one of them is awestruck and impressed with his intelligence and education. They think he's a prince who will rescue them, and every last one is certain he'll divorce you and stick a rock on their finger."

Camille clenched her small fists in her lap. "He really is a bastard."

Oliver raised an eyebrow. "You're just realizing that after twenty-nine years? What are you going to say when he knocks up one of his sweet young things? It hasn't happened yet—" he paused, placed extra emphasis on his next words "—that we know of, but unless he's gotten snipped, sooner or later, it will. His latest choices are younger, more determined, and we all know the way to a man's wallet is through his offspring—legitimate or not."

"Do you really think that's a possibility?"

He didn't miss the fear and humiliation on her face. "I think it's inevitable. Who knows? There could have been pregnancies we didn't know about that ended before you found out."

"Sometimes I have dreams about him fathering children all over town. I'm walking down the street and there's a row of women holding babies and small children, and every child has Carter's face." Camille leaned forward, clasped his hand. "Oliver, what kind of nut job am I to have dreams like that?"

He patted his sister's hand, said in the voice he'd used when they were children and she'd scraped her knees, "You're not the nut job; he is. But the longer you stay with him, the more you'll lose your grasp on reality and your beliefs. Did you ever think growing up that you'd find it acceptable for your husband to have affairs as long as he didn't get the woman pregnant? I'm sure you didn't, and yet that's what you're accepting. And what about the kids? What kind of message have you sent them? Victoria will believe she has to accept this behavior from her husband, while Simon might think he can cheat on his wife as long as he doesn't get his mistress pregnant."

She dabbed at her eyes with her lace handkerchief, murmured, "I've ruined their lives."

"Of course, you haven't, but I think you need to set an example for them."

"An example?" She shook her head. "The only example I can set is what *not* to do."

"It's never too late, Cammie. One step at a time." He closed his hands over hers. "I'll help if you like."

Her face lit up, and she looked like the young, hopeful school-girl she'd once been who was going to conquer the world, one good deed at a time. "You always know what to say, even if it's not what I want to hear. Thank you for being a great listener and a great brother."

"Welcome. You've got a lot going for you, but you've got to

take the first step. Maybe a baby step, but make sure you're moving forward."

"Okay. Baby steps. I can do that."

"Nobody can tell you whether to stay married or not. You need to think about your choice and why you're making it. Don't stay because you're afraid to leave, and don't leave because everybody tells you to…it's your choice. We all fall before we pick ourselves up and find a new path. But it's got to be *your* path." He smiled at her. "Now tell me, did you meet with a divorce attorney in New York?"

"What?"

That seemed to fluster her, so Oliver guessed the answer was no, but he had to find out. "You've been making trips to New York, and I was wondering if you consulted a divorce attorney."

The blush said she'd definitely been doing something she didn't want him to know about, though consulting an attorney might not have been it. She shook her head. "No attorney."

"Well? Plan on telling me what you were doing that's got you all red in the face?"

She looked away, shrugged. "Just being foolish, I guess."

Hmm. That could mean anything. "How foolish?"

Camille inched her gaze to his, mumbled, "I met with a plastic surgeon. He said he could tweak a few things, make me look younger." Pause. "More vibrant."

"So you can keep Carter's interest?"

The half shrug said maybe, maybe not. But when she spoke, the real answer sat between them. "So I can compete. What man wants a fifty-two-year-old with wrinkles, spider veins, and a saggy bottom?"

"No saggy boobs?" Oliver smiled at her deadpan stare. "Sorry, but fixing saggy boobs seems to be in every plastic surgeon's bag of tricks."

Camille puffed out her chest, glanced down at her small chest. "Maybe I'll add that to my list."

Oliver's smile faded. "How about you erase all of those fixes *and* the plastic surgeon from your list? You don't need any of them, Cammie. Work on you. *The real you.*" He pointed to her chest and her head. "The Camille that's inside, the one that's been hiding for too many years. That's the one people will love."

JENNIFER MERRICK never imagined Oliver Donovan sitting in her living room sipping oolong tea and nibbling on a banana nut muffin, but here he was, looking relaxed in his faded jeans and Led Zeppelin T-shirt, his feet in sandals, the gold hoop glinting in his left ear. When he spotted her watching him, he smiled. Why hadn't she ever realized how attractive he was? Those blue eyes did something to her insides when they looked at her, and when he spoke, the gentleness of his tone calmed her. Actually, his presence calmed her. Even now, with Lester Conroy sitting across from her, his lanky body folded into the Queen Anne chair Camille had gifted her years ago, she felt calm. She and Oliver had practiced her speech, talked about possible outcomes, and what she really wanted out of this conversation. *The past is the past, Jen. People make mistakes, hurt each other, wish like hell they could take it back. This is your chance to have a relationship with your mother again, let her get to know Hope. But it's got to be your decision.*

"Mr. Conroy, thank you for making another trip to Reunion Gap. I'm sorry I couldn't give you an answer during your last visit, but I've thought a lot about what you said." She paused, cleared her throat. "Especially the part about not blaming my mother for the parts of my life that haven't worked out the way I wanted them to. You're right, that's on me. It was easy to tell myself she turned me into an angry, untrusting person who looks at life as a chore to get through, rather than a joy to experience." She slid a look at Oliver, who nodded encouragement, and went on, "It's time I owned up to my choices as *my* choices, not anyone else's; the good *and* the bad. When I think about seeing my mother again, I wonder if she'll recognize me. I don't mean the physical appearance, because other than a few years and a few pounds, I still look the same, but I'm nothing like the foolish girl who left Magdalena ten years ago." She jabbed a finger at her chest. "Inside, I'm not that person anymore. I'm scarred and hurt, I don't trust well and have a hard time believing I deserve good things to happen to me." Her voice cracked, but she pushed on. "I'm working on that, but it's a process that's bound to have setbacks." She sniffed. "I'm afraid I might be a huge disappointment to a woman who found joy in the everyday and called life magical."

Oliver clasped her hand, held tight. "One day at a time, Jen."

She sniffed again, nodded. Oliver had given her a lavender-colored notebook with the photo of an orchid on the cover. He called it her gratitude journal and told her before she went to bed at night, he wanted her to list ten things she was grateful for…last night, she'd thought of twenty-three…

Lester Conroy toyed with his Stetson. "Your mother is one of the most generous people I've ever met. Kind-hearted, resilient, determined to find the best in others. But when she talks about you, she's not blaming the young girl who left, or what that girl did or said. You know who Mimi's blames? She blames herself."

Jennifer fought past the ache in her chest, pushed out the truth. "It's not her fault. She was trying to protect me from a situation I didn't want to see." The rest of the truth spilled out for the first time since she left Magdalena. "I'm responsible for damaging the relationship with my mother, and I'm the one who has to fix it. I don't think I'll ever forgive myself for not being there when my father got sick. I never said goodbye to him." Three sniffs. "I don't want to have that same regret with my mother."

The older man's thin lips pulled into a generous smile. "What would you like me to tell her?"

"Tell her I'll be in touch." That sounded cold and impersonal, like the old Jennifer Merrick who shielded her heart and wouldn't let anyone in. Did she really want to be that person? Wasn't she tired of the mistrust and the lack of joy? Yes, yes she was! "Tell my mother I'll come to Magdalena as soon as I can make arrangements for someone to watch the inn. Tell her she has a granddaughter named Hope who's coming with me." Her voice grew soft, filled with hope for a new beginning. "And tell her I love her."

Lester Conroy nodded. "I can certainly do that."

Oliver squeezed her hand, said in a gentle voice, "Mr. Conroy can tell your mother, or you can write a note and tell her yourself. What do you think about that?"

Jennifer turned to him, threw her arms around his neck and hugged him. He knew she wasn't ready for a phone call, but he also knew a letter was one step closer to that call, and more personal than a third-party relaying an emotional message. "Thank you, Oliver. Thank you for being here for me." She eased away, asked him the question she'd been holding close since she decided to visit her mother. "Will you come with us to Magdalena?" Asking that question left her exposed and vulnerable—it was a leap of faith and she'd jumped.

The answer came in the brightness of his blue eyes, seconds before he touched her cheek and said, "Of course."

～

ELIZABETH SAT in Rogan's back yard, re-creating a dark pink

hydrangea bloom on her sketchpad. The bloom possessed one of the most brilliant hues she'd ever seen. And yesterday, she'd captured the magnificent vibrancy of a lavender butterfly bush. The day before that it had been a purple and white columbine. Were the colors in Reunion Gap more exquisite than any other place she'd been, or was there another reason attached to her newfound sensory experiences? And was that other reason Rogan Donovan?

A rush of emotion surged through her, settled in her chest. There was no use denying her world was bigger, brighter, *happier* since she met Rogan. She was alive in a way she'd never been before, her heart open to the possibility of love, her soul ready to trust. Had she ever felt this way before, ever ventured into such foreign territory where she put her faith in someone else?

The answer was easy: no. There'd never been anyone she cared about enough to risk love or trust. Until Rogan. He made her *want* to trust him, made her want to believe in love and second chances. She still grew queasy when she thought of the reason their paths had crossed at all. If their fathers hadn't been tied together in a backstory of deceit and betrayal, Elizabeth and Rogan never would have met, never would have had the opportunity to fall in love. And whether or not they'd spoken the words, they *were* in love. It was only a matter of time before the words followed the feelings.

Perhaps she'd tell him tonight. *I love you, Rogan Donovan.* She smiled, her heart so full she knew it would burst if she didn't get the words out soon. Yes, tonight she would tell him.

"Elizabeth?"

The male voice startled her. She turned and recognized Tate Alexander, Camille's nephew. She'd run into him around town a few times and he'd always been charming and friendly, but at the moment, he looked neither. "Hello, Tate. I'm sorry, but Rogan isn't here. I don't expect him for another few hours." He really was very nice-looking...hadn't Camille said something about him and Charlotte? Or had that only been wishful thinking?

"Actually, I was looking for you." He moved closer, his tall figure blocking the sun as he stood over her, expression grim, lips unsmiling.

"Is something wrong?"

The silver eyes half the women in town called mesmerizing turned to ice, matched the tone in his next words. "Rogan's a good man, Elizabeth. He's honest, sincere, and loyal. I'm not going to stand by and watch him get stampeded by a lie he didn't see coming."

Why was he looking at her like that, as though she were the one carrying the lie that would hurt the man she loved? "What are you talking about?"

He reached into his shirt pocket, pulled out a folded piece of paper. "I found this in my father's bottom desk drawer four days ago. I almost missed it. Who would think the truth would be buried in an old-school planner? It was the planner that caught my attention. My father was such a stickler for making appoint-ments." Tate rubbed his jaw, his silver eyes narrowed. "Did you know some people make appointments to buy their mistresses presents? Yup, that's what he did. 'Ruby bracelet for Fiona' was listed in April, 'Spa day for Monique was September' and guess what was under October in handwriting so small it was hard to read?" Of course, he didn't expect an answer and plowed on as though he hadn't asked the question, "That was the real teller. 'Anniversary.' That's it. No gift mentioned, not number of years, nothing."

"I'm sorry, Tate. It must be very hard for you." She knew all about parents disappointing their children. Hadn't she lived her whole life in the shadow of her mother and the absent-minded affection of her father? But what did all of this have to do with her, and why was Tate looking at her like he was about to reveal a huge secret and she was smack in the middle of it?

"It is hard. It's messed up, actually, but I didn't come to talk about my screwed-up family life." He let out a quiet sigh, unfolded the piece of paper and handed it to her. "*This* is what I came to talk about."

He watched as she scanned the lines. *Phillip, our business is concluded. I ask that you refrain from further contact for the fore-seeable future. Should I require your services again, I'll contact you. Best Regards, Harrison Alexander.* She glanced up from the paper, met Tate's hard gaze. *He knew who she was!* But how? And how could she convince him to remain quiet about her true identity until she had a chance to tell Rogan? Elizabeth opted for ignorance. It might not work, but she had to try. She erased the emotion from her voice and looked him straight in the eye when she spoke. "Who's Phillip and what does this mean?"

He reached into his pocket, pulled out a folded envelope, pointed to the address on the front. "Do you know there's a woman in the same town as Phillip Hayes who's also an artist?" He rubbed his jaw, studied her. "What are the odds?"

"Tate—"

"Her name's Elizabeth Hayes, though, not Elizabeth Hastings, like you, but close. I hope she's not one of those copycat types trying to pretend she's you." His words suffocated her, made her lightheaded. "Imagine somebody pretending they weren't who they said they were? Unforgiveable, don't you think?"

"How do you know this?"

His lips pulled into a slow smile. "The Internet is a fascinating treasure trove of information. You can discover a lot if you start reading the obituaries they post. I highly recommend it. Seems this artist named Elizabeth Hayes lost her parents in a small-plane crash a few months ago."

What to say to that? "How sad."

He crossed his arms over his chest and shook his head. "You are one tough cookie, Elizabeth *Hayes*, I'll give you that."

"Please—"

"Please what? Keep quiet while you take advantage of one of the most decent guys I've ever known?"

"I would never take advantage of him. Why are you doing this?"

"Because I want to protect him. Contrary to what you might have heard, not all Alexanders are cheaters and swindlers. Some of us really do want to do the right thing." He scowled, said in a harsh voice, "Some of us even want to right a few wrongs. Take the deal Gordon T. Haywood, I mean, your *father*, made with Rogan's father. Bad deal, right? Actually, from what I heard, it was a disaster; ruined the man's credibility, and in the end, ruined the man. I knew something didn't sound right about that deal and when I got full access to the company's files after my old man's stroke, I started doing a little digging. Amazing what you can learn when the head honcho's out of the picture and you've been away for a few years. Gives you a whole new perspective on things."

"I didn't know…"

"Didn't know what? That your father was planning to destroy Jonathan Donovan? Or that Harrison Alexander helped bankroll that destruction? I've got copies of four cancelled checks from my father to yours. Care to tell me about them?"

"I don't know about the checks and I didn't know he planned to cheat anyone." Her voice cracked, split open. "I swear."

His expression said he thought she was lying. "Fine, so you didn't know. But you *did* know something or you wouldn't have landed in Reunion Gap under an assumed name, and you wouldn't have targeted the son of the victim."

"I didn't target Rogan." Yes, she'd wanted to meet him so she could figure out a way to help him and his family, but entering into a relationship with him? Falling in love? That had never been part of any plan. It had simply happened.

"What would you call it then? Relieving guilt? Making up for Daddy's bad deeds?" He stared at her, jaw clenched. "Tell me, damn it, or I swear I'll call Rogan now and tell him the whole sordid truth about how far you'll go to play this little game of yours."

"It's not a game." Her voice dipped, fell out in a whisper of misery and regret. "I want to help him. I want to help everyone my father hurt. That's the reason I came here."

"Sure it is."

Of course, he didn't believe her. "What other reason could I possibly have?"

"Maybe you wanted to follow your old man's course of destruction and see who else you could take down." He rubbed his jaw as if considering the many possibilities. "Or maybe your intentions are more sadistic in nature. Yeah, maybe you wanted an up-close view and personal look into the life of the family your father tried to destroy."

"No." She shook her head. "No," she repeated. "I told you, I never knew about any of this, not until after he died." She hadn't planned to mention Uncle Everett's role in this, but now it seemed necessary. "My father's business partner told me. He said he's been donating money to people in this town for years. Anonymously, of course."

"Of course. And what about the Donovans? Did he donate money to them, like a cause, or maybe to the Alexanders, like hush money?"

"He didn't give the Alexanders money and he couldn't give the Donovans any because he said they had a tight control on their finances, including their debt."

"Thanks to him and your father. So, this guy you're telling me about had a burst of conscience and wanted to make things right. That's where you come in?"

"Yes. He wanted me to come here and make good on the deal they cheated Rogan's father out of with JD Manufacturing."

Tate Alexander looked at her with a mix of disbelief and disgust. "Nice plan. So, you butter up Rogan, get him to fall for you, and then what? You do the deal and find a way to screw the Donovans again?"

"We do the deal and do right by them."

"And when do you tell Rogan you aren't just an artist, but the daughter of the man who took everything from his family? Do you slide that in between coffee and dessert or do you wait until after the kids start coming?"

She'd been battling this same question herself. Rogan deserved to know, *needed* to know, but when and how? That was the issue. There'd been no good answer, but Tate Alexander wouldn't want to hear that. He'd want a timeline and details. "I'm going to tell him."

"Yes, you are. But not yet." He gave her a slow smile that chilled her. "You're not going to tell him until renovations for JD Manufacturing are underway. I'll match whatever you're putting up, the more money, the quicker we can get moving. I've got a limited time to make retribution and that means I need to move on the rebuild. Who knows when my father will recover enough to take over again? It could happen soon, or never. I'm not going to take the chance that Rogan and his family don't get what should have been theirs."

Elizabeth agreed with everything he said, except the part about waiting to tell the man she loved who she really was. "If I tell Rogan now, he'll be angry, but at least I'll have a chance that he'll forgive me. What you're asking is that I stay quiet for a few more months." Her voice wobbled. "I can't do that."

"I don't think I really gave you a choice now, did I?"

"Are you trying to blackmail me?"

"Me? Blackmail you?" He laughed. "That's rich, Elizabeth, coming from a family of blackmailers. I'm not trying to do anything but appeal to your sense of right and wrong. If you confess now, Rogan will kill the deal. He'd rather go down than take dirty money."

Lies on top of lies. She hated making up stories about who she was and why she was here. All she wanted to do was tell Rogan the truth. He deserved that much.

And yet, she wanted him to have his building, to honor his father this way. How could she jeopardize his chance to see his father vindicated?

"Well? Are you in this with me or do you want to fly solo?"

Elizabeth dragged her gaze to his. "I love him, Tate."

"Do you now?"

She nodded, tried to keep the tears from falling. Whatever had happened to Tate Alexander had left him scarred, distrustful of women and the motives in their relationships. "Some woman hurt you, didn't she? That's why you don't want to trust any of us."

His silver gaze turned to soot, burned her. "I don't like games or lies, especially when it has to do with a relationship. Show a little selfless love, Elizabeth. Are you capable of that? Pump the money into Rogan's business and keep quiet until the deal's done. Then you can sing him a sonnet, bake him a pie, and tell him he rocks your world." He paused, rubbed his jaw. "And then you can tell him Gordon T. Haywood was your father."

12

Two months later

Elizabeth found Rose in the living room, her dark hair illuminated by the afternoon sun, head bent in concentration as she worked on her latest project. Delicate lace rested beside her as she created a unique design for her latest bridal handkerchief. "It's going to be beautiful."

The woman glanced up, an expression of joy and peace on her face. "Yes, it is." Her eyes grew bright, her voice soft, as she leaned forward, whispered, "It's for you."

Heat swirled through Elizabeth, made her dizzy. "Me?"

"A mother always knows," she said. "You and Rogan are in love. It's obvious, and it's wonderful. There's nothing more magical than love. Don't let it escape you, no matter what." She clasped Elizabeth's hand, squeezed. "Once it's gone, you'll spend the rest of your life wishing you could get it back."

She spoke as though she'd experienced this kind of loss. Was she talking about Rogan's father, Jonathan? Or had she loved and lost someone before him? "You've known this kind of loss, haven't you?"

"I have." The words slid from her lips to spill through the room and settle between them like a mournful song of love and loss. "Indeed, I have. And that's why I want to spare you. No matter the differences between you and my son, work them out. Don't let pride or fear put it at risk."

Elizabeth recalled Rose's words later that evening as she drove to JD Manufacturing to help Rogan with inventory. In less than six days, the factory would open and Jonathan Donovan's dream would be realized. At last. She parked the SUV and grabbed the bag from the Cherry Top Diner containing two turkey clubs, side salads, and a slice of cherry pie for Rogan. They'd decided to work through dinner in the hopes they could finish early enough to have a night together. He hadn't slept in her bed in three days and she missed him, missed the sound of his breathing…the feel of him against her naked skin…

"Rogan? I brought your favorite dessert." She slipped through the door, made her way to his office. The place was a lot different from the first time she saw it. The machines, the workbenches, the tools made it come alive and soon machinists would be sawing, turning, and sanding. Before she came to Reunion Gap, she'd never been inside a manufacturing plant. Now, she knew the difference between jointing and planing, what mortise and tenon meant, and how to calculate run times.

Intriguing and fascinating.

Like Rogan Donovan.

She rounded the corner, took the final steps to his office. "I hope you're hungry, because…" She blinked. Stared. Blinked again. "Uncle Everett? What…what are you doing here?"

"Hello, dear." He ignored her question and moved toward her, gave her a big hug and a peck on the cheek. "Rogan and I were having a conversation." A smile pulled from his thin lips. "He's an impressive young man; I can certainly see why you're so taken with him."

She slid her gaze to Rogan who was trying very hard not to smile. Or maybe he was trying not to laugh? That didn't seem like the response of a man who'd just found out the woman he was involved with had been keeping secrets from him. Elizabeth moved toward him. "Hi."

"Hi." Those lips she'd tasted many times morphed into a full-blown smile. "I was just telling your uncle you were bringing dinner." He gave her a quick kiss on the mouth, then glanced at the bag. "We knew it wouldn't be homemade, but we were taking bets on the cuisine."

"Indeed we were." Uncle Everett sniffed the bag. "I don't smell pasta primavera. That was my guess."

Rogan laughed, snatched the bag, and peeked inside. "I said meatball subs."

"Turkey clubs with avocado. Side salads. Cherry pie for you." She took the bag from him, set it on the table and proceeded to remove the contents. What on earth was her uncle doing here? She'd never told him about her conversation with Tate Alexander two months ago, and as far as he knew, everything was moving along as planned. There had been one thing she'd wanted him to know, and two nights ago, she'd told him.

You...you're seeing Rogan Donovan? Pause. *Romantically?*

Yes.

Oh. Another pause, this one followed by a tightness in his next words. *Is that wise?*

Wise? What do you mean?

He doesn't know who you are. Don't you think that's a bit...risky?

I'm going to tell him. Soon.

And then what?

What do you mean?

Once you tell him the truth, what could you possibly hope to gain? Why would you do it? Why not just leave things as they are?

Because I want him to know the truth.

Can't you let him believe you're somebody else? What difference could it make once you're gone?

But don't you see, Uncle Everett? I don't want to leave. I want to stay. Here, with Rogan. I want to make a life with him. I love him.

"So, your uncle called yesterday and said he wanted to check out the town you couldn't seem to stop talking about."

Yesterday? "Really? I'm surprised you didn't tell me."

Rogan smiled at her. "Everett wanted to surprise you. It was hard keeping a secret from you, but he said it would be worth it." His voice dipped, filled with gentleness. "Are you surprised?"

Oh, she was surprised all right, but not in a good way. She nodded, slid a look at her uncle who'd developed a sudden interest in the stripes on his tie. "Surprised isn't the word."

"Good. Then it was worth a bit of subterfuge to keep the secret."

Talk of subterfuge and secrets made her stomach flip-flop. Elizabeth unwrapped her turkey club sandwich and extended a square to her uncle. "Would you like to share?"

"I am a tad hungry." He adjusted his glasses, accepted the sandwich. "Thank you, dear. What would I do without you?"

The next hour was filled with a mix of anxiety and dread as the conversation hopscotched from her childhood to Rogan's, their parents, the siblings she'd always wanted, the life he left in California, and ended with Uncle Everett's jovial comments about overcoming adversity and finding each other in a town no bigger than a dot on the map.

"How curious that you two found one another. Fate was no doubt at work, but imagine the odds?" Uncle Everett dabbed his thin lips with a paper napkin. "We're both accountants, Rogan, but I'm not sure we could calculate the odds on that one."

Rogan nodded. "No idea." He lifted the lid off the slice of cherry pie. "Let me grab a few forks and we can share this pie. Be right back."

When Elizabeth was certain he was out of earshot, she turned to her uncle, whispered, "What are you doing here?"

He tilted his head to one side as though he had no idea what she was talking about. "I told you, dear. I wanted to see the place and the person who—"

"You can't stay here. It's too dangerous."

"It was too dangerous the second you got involved with him on a personal level." His brown eyes filled with sadness. "We can only hope he's a man with a generous heart and a capacity for forgiveness."

"I'm going to tell him the truth. Very soon."

Tsk-tsk. "You were supposed to facilitate a deal that would pay our debt to his family and right the wrong done to him, not fall in love with him."

"I didn't plan on what happened between us. It just happened."

"Take it from a man who has walked this earth a lot of years, nothing *just* happens, Elizabeth. Everything occurs in the universe for a reason, good or bad, and we usually have a hand in it, whether we like to admit it or not."

"Can we talk about this later?" She glanced toward the office door, heard Rogan's footsteps.

"Of course. I'm not in a rush."

"I want you to leave tomorrow."

He patted her hand, offered a half smile and said, "I'll protect you. Trust me."

Before she could ask what he meant, Rogan bounded into the

office, tossed two forks on the table. "Here we go. You've got to try this pie, Everett. It's even better than my mother's."

Her uncle forked a hunk of cherry pie. "Too bad Elizabeth doesn't bake."

"She's got other attributes that more than make up for it," Rogan said, reaching out to stroke her arm.

"Thank you." She forced herself to nibble on a bite of pie. All she wanted to do was get her uncle out of here, away from Rogan and the chance that the man she loved might find out her true identity before she could tell him herself. The smile Rogan gave her spoke of trust and commitment. And love? Yes, maybe that, too.

And she would do anything to protect that.

ROGAN POURED TWO SCOTCHES, handed one to Everett. "To the future." He clinked glasses with Elizabeth's uncle, sipped his scotch. He hadn't wanted to celebrate the future in a long time, but things were different now, and it had all started when Elizabeth walked into his life. Everett was right; the odds of that happening weren't even calculable, but then fate wasn't something you could analyze.

"I can't tell you how pleased I am to see my niece happy." The older man's eyes misted behind his horn-rimmed glasses. "She deserves to be with someone who cares about her. Life hasn't always been kind to her, no matter how hard she tried." He cleared his throat. "Did she tell you her parents were so involved with each other, they never had time for her? She was more of an inconvenience to them, which is how I got involved and earned the title of uncle."

"Elizabeth mentioned that her parents were emotionally

distant." Why have a child if you didn't want to be involved in its life? He hated thinking of the woman he cared about withdrawn, desperate for affection. He'd make damn sure she never felt that way again.

"Emotionally distant?" Everett attempted a smile that fell flat. "That's a very proper term for horrible parents, isn't it?"

Rogan shrugged. "In a way, I guess it is."

"My niece has struggled with attachments in the past. She's always been an outsider, unwilling to let strangers in or her real feelings out. But I can tell she cares about you, Rogan. She cares about you a great deal."

His chest ached with the need to protect her, take care of her...love her. He opened his mouth and let bits of truth slip out. "I care about her a great deal, too." *Like a ring and forever-after type of care.*

"That much is obvious. I'm not so old that I don't recognize love when I see it, and you two are either on your way or already there." He raised a brow, tapped a finger against his chin. "Wouldn't you agree?"

So, the guy knew Rogan and Elizabeth weren't short-term? Then he'd probably also figured out his niece might end up staying in Reunion Gap. Permanently. But Rogan wasn't saying anything until he and Elizabeth had the talk that included words like *future, commitment,* and, of course, *love.* Yeah, he guessed it was time to have that talk and tonight felt like the right time. Just as soon as he finished his scotch, he could say goodnight to Everett and head over to the Peace & Harmony Inn where he'd spill his heart to the woman who owned it and hope she felt the same way. Rogan worked up a smile and eyed the man. "Let's just say that you might be on to something."

Everett removed his glasses, pulled out a handkerchief, and dabbed his eyes. "If I have to give her up, I want to know you'll stand by her, no matter what."

"You mean like in sickness and all that?" Was the guy angling for a proposal commitment for his niece? Rogan sighed. What the hell. Why not admit the truth since the guy already knew what was happening next? "Yeah, I'm all-in if that's what you're asking, but I don't want to say more until I speak with Elizabeth."

"I understand." Everett dabbed his eyes once more, put his glasses on, squinted twice. "Do you believe in unconditional love, Rogan?"

Unconditional love? "You mean, like loving someone without judgment or expectation?" He thought of Elizabeth, her smile, the way her voice calmed him. Would he love her, no matter what? The answer burst from him before he could yank it back and examine its implications. "Yeah, I guess I do."

"Good. That's exactly what I'd hoped to hear because you're going to need that for what I'm about to tell you." He sipped the last of his scotch, set it on the workbench. "You see, sometimes people do the wrong thing for the right reason. They behave in a manner that's unlike them. Perhaps they withhold the truth or fabricate a story because they believe in the outcome. It's not who they are, but in these circumstances, it's what they do."

Rogan stared at him, gaze narrowed. "I have no idea what you're talking about, but if this has to do with Elizabeth in any way, or if she's in some kind of danger, you'd better tell me right now."

"The only danger to Elizabeth is how you'll react when I tell you the truth."

"The truth? What truth?" The beginnings of a headache pounded his left temple. "What truth?"

"Elizabeth's presence in Reunion Gap is not fate or divine intervention. She's here because I asked her to come and repair the damage her father and I committed when we cheated yours. Her real name is Elizabeth Hayes. Phillip Hayes was her father, though you probably knew him as Gordon T. Haywood."

Of all the betrayals he'd ever endured, including the loss of a fiancée and the scheming of the Alexanders, he'd never suffered a greater one than Elizabeth's. She'd known the pitiful story that was his life and his family's long before she ventured to Reunion Gap. She'd even known the person responsible for the disaster, and she hadn't said a single word. Not. One. Word. She'd smiled and played the demure, lonely sophisticate, a woman who wanted to be accepted, understood, liked for herself.

What a scammer!

He'd fallen for it because he'd been desperate to believe her. What was it about her that pulled him in, made him reckless, made him ignore the signs that said she might not be exactly who she said she was? He'd asked a few questions at first, tried to remain aloof, but the pull had been too great, and he'd succumbed to it.

Had she known that's what would happen? Had that been her plan all along?

When Everett left him a short while ago, he'd begged Rogan to employ the unconditional love he professed to believe in and try to view Elizabeth's actions as those of a person who lied and deceived for a noble cause. If he were able to find it in his heart to do that, the man insisted Rogan could forgive his niece. Not only that, his trust in her would grow, as would his love.

Right. Was this guy for real? The only thing Rogan wanted from the woman who'd deceived him was a confession—eye to eye— and then he'd boot her out of town and try to bury the worst mistake he'd ever made in his life. He parked his car at the inn, bounded up the front steps, and slipped inside. Jennifer Merrick had given him permission to come and go without the courtesy of a knock. Tonight, he was glad for this privilege. Tomorrow, he'd compose a script when people asked about Elizabeth's departure that included words like *unsuitable, bad timing,* and *short-term*. If they persisted with their inquiries, he'd toss out the conversation killer: *no comment*.

He knocked on her door, opened it when her soft voice invited him in. For just a second, he let himself forget her lies and treachery and soaked in the beauty of the woman who had calmed him, given him hope and moments of pure joy. That was all over now, smashed with her uncle's words as he tried to protect her from the impending fallout. Did the man really believe it would be as easy as employing a "forgive and forget" mantra?

Elizabeth lay sprawled on the bed, sketchpad open, pencils beside her in an art box. She offered him a tentative smile and sat up. "I should have told you my uncle nurses his drinks." She eased off the bed, moved toward him in a T-shirt and black underwear. "I was starting to get worried about you."

Any other night, the T-shirt and underwear would be on the floor in less than ten seconds. Not tonight. Not ever again. "Why would you be worried?" He kept his gaze trained on her, intent on finding the exact second that the lie would take over.

She shrugged, placed her small hands on his shoulders, leaned on tiptoe to kiss him. "I always worry about you," she whispered against his lips. "That's what people do who care about each other."

Rogan caught her wrists, stepped back—away from her and the life he thought they'd have. He spotted the second she figured out he knew the truth about her. Those lips he'd devoured so many times began to quiver, her eyes glistened, and the expression on her face spoke of such regret and sorrow it almost made him forget why they could never be together.

"Rogan." She moved toward him, but he held up a hand, backed away.

"Stop. Just stop." He dragged both hands over his face, stared at her. "We're strangers, Elizabeth. That's all we really are to each other."

"No, that's not true." She hugged her middle, shook her head. "We're so much more than that. You *know* we are."

"Do I?" He let out a soft laugh that scorched his throat. "Was anything about us true? Or were we just another part of a scheme, like your father's was? He destroyed a Donovan, maybe you thought you'd try your hand at it, too?"

"It was never that way. If you believe nothing else about me, please believe that I only wanted to help your family. After my parents died, Uncle Everett told me what happened. He admitted his part in deceiving your father and said he'd found a way to make things right, but he needed my help. He said we owed your family." Elizabeth's voice cracked, thinned. "I hated the thought of deceiving innocent people, but I hated what my father had done to them even more. And then I met you."

"Yeah, and then you met me." He did not want to hear the sadness in her voice, see the pain on her face. He wanted to block it all out, forget she ever meant anything to him.

But how the hell was he going to do that when she was in every breath he took, when she lived in his damn soul? "How long until you told me the truth? Or would you have kept that lie from me until the truth and lies all blended together and you couldn't tell them apart?"

She shook her head. "No. I was trying to find the right time to tell you."

"The right time, huh? How about before I had to find out myself? That would have been a good time."

"Do you think I don't know that? I was scared." She paused, licked her lips. "I didn't want to risk jeopardizing whatever was going on between us. It was too important, too powerful." Her voice dipped. "I love you, Rogan. I couldn't risk losing you."

His laughter swirled around them, cold, brutal. "You pretty much torched whatever we had; trust me on that."

"Don't say that." She clasped his arm. "Please don't say that."

Rogan lifted her hand from his arm, stepped back. "Whether I say it or not doesn't change the facts. Whatever we had is over. You killed it with your lies."

He made it to the door, had his hand on the knob before she said the words that would change their lives. "I'm pregnant."

13

Three days passed without a word from Rogan.

Nothing.

When she told him she was pregnant, he'd turned and stared at her, so long and hard she'd had to look away.

Then he was gone.

She'd cried the rest of the night and the day after that, staying in her room until Jennifer found her huddled in bed with the comforter tucked under her chin. The whole sordid tale spilled out then: who her father was, what he'd done, what she'd done, and ended with the pregnancy announcement. Jennifer listened, one hand stroking Elizabeth's back, the other handing her tissues as the tears flowed.

Worse things have happened to couples, she'd said. *You two love each other. You'll get through this, start a life together with the baby.*

No, that's not going to happen. Rogan isn't going to forgive, and he's never going to give me a second chance. I saw it in his eyes. It's over.

But what about the baby?

I don't know. More tears. *I just don't know.*

A pause, a catch of her breath, followed by, *You are going to keep it, aren't you?*

Yes. A ragged sigh. *Absolutely.*

When she was young, she'd assumed one day she'd marry and have a family. As she got older and the relationships didn't develop, or fizzled out soon after they'd begun, she stopped thinking about husbands or children. But Rogan Donovan changed everything. He'd made her believe anything was possible.

And now that belief was gone.

On the afternoon of the third day after her world fell apart, Elizabeth showered, dressed, and made her way to the kitchen for green tea and cinnamon toast. Jennifer shared a secret of her own yesterday, one that explained why she wanted to help Elizabeth. When Jennifer arrived in Reunion Gap ten years ago, she was all alone, estranged from her family, abandoned by her new husband, and pregnant. The owner of the Peace & Harmony Inn took her in and helped her adjust to a life she hadn't anticipated, one that included a pregnancy, and later, a new baby. Jennifer said it was time to give back and that's exactly what she planned to do.

Of course, the woman believed Rogan would get over his hurt and pledge his love for Elizabeth. But that was doubtful, and something in the way Jennifer's voice quivered when she spoke the words told Elizabeth she thought so, too.

"I won't tell anyone, not even Oliver," Jennifer said, as she slid another piece of cinnamon toast onto a plate and handed it to her.

"Thank you." The whole town would start buzzing soon with comments and theories on what happened between one of the most sought-after bachelors in town and the new girl.

Nobody's going to tie Rogan Donovan down, especially an outsider.

I knew he'd never marry her.

I thought she might be the one.

Me, too.

Never.

But what happened?

Who knows?

Who cares? He's on the market again.

One more chance to win him over.

Elizabeth would ignore them all, just like she used to when children called her clumsy and much too shy. But what would she do about the baby? Where would she go? Could she really live in Reunion Gap, see Rogan on the street, and treat him as though they'd never been more to one another than casual acquaintances?

Could *he* do that?

And what if he wanted to be part of the baby's life? Would they get involved with the shared parenting she'd heard about, work out schedules and later, school pick-up and drop-offs? It was so foreign, but people did it all the time. At least, she'd read that they did. But what did she really know about any of it?

Absolutely nothing.

And that was terrifying.

She placed a hand over her belly. If she hadn't missed two periods, she wouldn't have thought about the possibility of pregnancy. Her periods had never been regular and the need for protection had been almost nonexistent.

Until Rogan.

Everything changed then, and condoms weren't effective if you only used them "some of the time." She'd been too caught up in the man and the emotion to consider the consequences of her actions. Well, now she'd have several months to adjust to those consequences—with or without the other half of the equation.

"What did your uncle say?"

Jennifer's gentle tone pulled her back. "He wants me to come home. He said he'll help any way he can." She worked up a smile as she recalled their conversation. "I guess he thinks he'd be a good babysitter. It's hard to think about that right now when I don't even feel pregnant. No nausea, no tiredness, nothing."

"And you're sure you are, right?"

Elizabeth lifted a brow. "I took the test three times. I'm pregnant."

"I really would like you to stay here. You could live at the inn, work from here, and I'd help out with the baby." Her blue eyes turned bright, glistened. "We could start a group for single mothers. I know a few in town and we could share our struggles."

"Maybe." Not that long ago, she'd let herself believe she and Rogan had a future together, one that included marriage and children. Well, they'd gotten the children part right, but not much else.

"Think about it when you make your decision."

"I will. Thank you." Elizabeth finished her tea, picked up her cup and plate and carried them to the sink. "I've got to visit Rose today. I can't put it off any longer; it's not fair to her,"

"Oh, she's going to take it hard, isn't she? Oliver told me she had you and Rogan walking down the aisle by Christmas."

Elizabeth shrugged, said in a quiet voice, "A lot of dreams aren't going to happen, especially that one." Jennifer must have sensed she didn't want to talk about her predicament any longer because she insisted Elizabeth call Rose and leave the cleanup to her.

Of course, Rose wanted to see her. *I've missed you, Elizabeth. Where have you been? I've been asking Rogan, but that boy can be so infuriating sometimes. He clammed up and told me you were very busy and didn't have time for a visit. Is that true? What have you been doing?*

I'll tell you all about it when I see you.

*Good, I'll look forward to it. And can you please make my son
smile? He's been in such a mood these past few days.*

She wanted to tell her that nothing she said could make her
son smile, and *she* was the reason for his mood, but she didn't.
Instead, she forced the emotion from her voice and agreed to meet
in an hour.

And now here she was, sitting in the Donovans' living room
with Rogan's mother, sipping a lemonade and making small talk
while she worked up to the real reason for her visit. Rose
Donovan deserved to know the truth about who Elizabeth really
was, and why she'd come to Reunion Gap. She also should know
that whatever hopes she may have had that Elizabeth and her son
would end up together were not going to happen. Ever. There
would come a time to tell her about the baby, but that would
happen after Rogan either accepted or rejected the idea of a
child.

"What on earth is going on with my son?" Rose frowned.
"Such a complete turnaround from these past few months. Do you
think it has to do with the opening of the factory? I hope not, but
it's hard to tell. Rogan's never been one to share his feelings,
though I'd have thought he'd share them with you." She offered a
smile, patted her hand. "I'll bet he shares more with you than he's
ever shared with any other woman."

What to say to that? It was time for the truth. "I know why
he's not happy, Rose. It's because of me."

"You?" Rose laughed, shook her dark head. "No, it could
never be you." Her eyes sparkled. "He's in love with you. The
way he talks about you is pure delight."

"Maybe that's how it was, but not now…not since he found
out the truth." *I will not cry. I will push out the words and I will
not cry.* But her heart ignored her brain as tears filled her eyes.
"I'm not who I said I was, and I didn't come here just to draw
flowers." She cleared her throat, clasped her hands so tight her

nails dug into her palms. "I came to right the wrong that was done to your husband and your family."

"I don't understand." Rose leaned toward her, touched her arm. "What are you trying to tell me?"

"The man who cheated your husband and ruined his name?" A tear slipped down her cheek, then another. "That man was my father."

The woman's hand slipped away from Elizabeth's arm. "No," she whispered. "It can't be."

"I'm so sorry, Rose. I never meant to hurt anyone, especially Rogan. When my uncle told me what happened with your family, he said there was a way to fulfill the deal my father made, and I could help, but it would mean hiding my true identity from all of you."

Rose lowered her head, began to sob. "No, dear Lord, no."

Elizabeth swiped at her tears. "My uncle made a surprise visit the other day and told Rogan the truth. I guess he thought love would prevail and Rogan would forgive me for the deception once he realized my motives were meant to help. That didn't happen." Her voice cracked. "Whatever we shared is over." *Except for the child you don't know about yet.*

"I OFTEN WONDER IF God is truly all-forgiving?" Rose's eyes misted, her words sprinkled with doubt. "I do hope so, because I have committed a grievous offense, Oliver, and I need Him to find it in his heart to forgive me because I cannot forgive myself."

His sister-in-law often rambled on about past injustices she'd committed, though he couldn't imagine a compassionate and giving woman like Rose doing anything to harm another. Still, she'd gotten herself into an agitated state and if she couldn't settle down soon, he'd have to call Rogan. The boy knew how to calm his mother, though right now, worry over him was at the center of her agitation.

Why couldn't Elizabeth have been who she said she was so Rogan could finally find a slice of happiness—and peace? Bad enough the woman stole his heart and then ripped it to shreds, but to lie about who she was? And worse, to lie about who her father was and why she was really here? Tears and "I'm sorry, I never wanted to hurt you" meant nothing when compared to the magnitude of the damage she'd done to that boy. As if he needed more pain and heartache.

"I think Elizabeth really wanted to help Rogan." Rose clutched a scrap of lace between her hands. "And I think she loved him, too. How tragic that a past injustice she had no claim over would destroy them." She stared at the lace, loosened her grip. "That sin is on me, Oliver."

He laid a hand on hers, gentled his voice, "Rose, I know you love your son, but you aren't to blame for what happened between Rogan and Elizabeth. She's the one who came to this town and lied to all of us. Despite her intentions, we Donovans don't take to liars. Didn't Jonathan always say that no matter how bad things were, he always wanted to know the truth? The truth was something he could handle, but finding out down the road that what he thought was the truth was just a lie?" He sighed, thought of the principles that had made his brother admired and later, ridiculed. Still, there'd never been a better or more honorable man than Jonathan Donovan, and if he were here right now, he'd have no sympathy for a woman who couldn't tell the truth, no matter how well intentioned the lie might be.

Rose dragged her gaze to his. "Jonathan was a good man." Pause. "Much too good for me."

Why would she say such a thing? Maybe he *should* call Rogan and tell him his mother was in a dark place and needed his help. "Why don't I call Rogan?" If anybody could help her, he could.

"No." She shook her head, twice. "I don't want him to hear what I'm about to tell you. There were so many times I wanted to tell Jonathan the truth, but I couldn't risk losing him, or worse, couldn't risk losing his love. In the end, I destroyed him."

"Rose—"

She held up a hand, her gaze determined, fierce. "Please. Let me tell you what I should have confessed to my husband years ago. Maybe once you know the truth, you'll help me find a way to save Rogan and Elizabeth."

Not likely. "I'm listening."

"After the commotion between Rogan and Elizabeth, she visited me, told me all about her parents, how she'd struggled most of her life to fit in, how her mother and father never had enough time for her. Do you know the only person who treated her with love and respect was her father's business partner, a man she considered her uncle though they were no blood relation?" She clasped the lace to her chest, clutched it so hard her knuckles lost their color. "I cannot imagine."

Oliver rubbed his jaw, settled back in his chair, and waited for more of the sob story. Elizabeth whatever her real last name was had a story that could wring out tears from half the town.

Not him, though.

He knew better.

Was any of her story true, or was it an attempt to toy with a sick woman's mind?

"The poor girl's tears choked the words from her, but she pushed on, and begged me to forgive her for lying to the town. I held my tongue, when what I really wanted to do was tell her how I'd been lying to everyone for years: my husband, my children, my friends. Do you know Gordon T. Haywood paid me a visit before he left town for good? He sat right here in this living room, sipping iced tea, a crocodile smile on his face, and told me he was going to rip apart Jonathan's integrity and honor, shred by shred. I couldn't understand why a man who'd pretended to be our friend could turn so vicious." Her lips trembled, eyes a mix of horror and pain. "But then he spoke again, and I knew exactly why he wanted to destroy Jonathan." She closed her eyes, blinked hard. "And *I* was the reason." Tears streamed down her cheeks, slipped to her chin, landed on her blouse. Her shoulders shook, her head dipped, but she tried to get out the words. "I…was the…reason. I killed him, Oliver, just as surely as if I'd pushed him off the ledge myself."

"Rose, that's not true." Oliver pulled her into his arms, tried to soothe her. "People are responsible for their own actions and the consequences that follow." He eased away from her, tipped her chin up so he could look into her eyes. "You couldn't have known what would happen and you certainly couldn't have prevented it." He offered a half smile. "We all have demons, nobody can fight them for us. I loved my brother, but he was a proud, unbending man, and I think that did him in."

"No." She shook her head, clutched his arms and dug her nails into his skin. "*I* did him in. It was me, Oliver." Rose cleared her throat, let go of her hold on him, and settled back in her chair. When she spoke again, her voice held an odd calmness to it that he hadn't heard in a long time. "A young woman visited Reunion Gap one summer. Blonde and beautiful, just out of college. Sophisticated. Wealthy, like a movie star. The whole town was captivated by her." She paused as if recalling the woman's arrival in Reunion Gap. "But no one was more entranced by her than Jonathan. He and I were friends, on the verge of becoming something more, when *she* arrived. It wasn't surprising that she was taken with him, or that within days, they were the talk of the town. *Wealthy, beautiful socialite meets down-to-earth hometown hero.* It was the stuff of storybooks. I was angry and hurt and feeling so very lonely. A woman questioning her own attractiveness and self-worth is an easy target." She sighed, her voice drifting back to a time years ago. "The closer Jonathan and this woman grew, the more desperate and uncertain I became. I made a very bad choice and before summer ended, I was left with the consequences."

When a woman talked about doubting her self-worth, making bad choices, and getting saddled with their consequences, Oliver thought of pregnancy. It hadn't taken a mathematician to calculate that Rogan's early arrival didn't add up to an appropriate amount of time following his parents' wedding. Sure, they'd tried the "premature birth" gig, but everybody knew Jonathan and Rose were "parents to be" before they said their "I do's."

So what? Who cared?

But what Rose had just told him made no sense. Who was the wealthy beauty queen who'd won over his brother? What happened to her? And what kind of target had Rose been, and for whom? Bad choices? Consequences? "You're speaking in code, Rose, and I'm sorry, but I can't figure it out. Can you translate for me, please, like tell me straight up what you're talking about?"

She hesitated, sucked in a breath, then another. "I told Jonathan she was cheating on him with Harrison Alexander. You know they couldn't stand each other, always pitting good against evil, right against wrong. Harrison was the perfect scapegoat, and I used him."

"Why?"

Her eyes grew bright, her expression fierce. "I had to save myself, Oliver, that's why. How could I let the whole town know what a fool I'd been?" Her breath turned choppy, her words uneven. "I made him believe she'd cheated on him with his enemy, a man who was engaged to be married. And then I slept with Jonathan, and two months later, I told him I was pregnant."

There were too many questions, smothered in deceit and

betrayal. If Rose had orchestrated such a grand scheme, there had to be a damn good reason, like a pregnancy by another man. The possibility made Oliver want to puke. "Were you pregnant by another man when you slept with my brother?" The dip of her head was so slight he might not have recognized it for a "yes" if he weren't looking for it. "Did Jonathan know?"

"He never knew."

"So, Rogan…" *Dear God, no.*

"He's not Jonathan's son." She paused, swiped at her cheeks. "But he *is* Jonathan's son in every way that matters. You know that, Oliver, surely you do."

He wished he'd never come here today. Why had his sister-in-law felt the sudden need to unburden herself when she'd held the secret close for so many years? What was he supposed to do with this information? Damn it, how was he supposed to look at his nephew without pity for what he didn't know, and anger for the truth that might escape one day? "Why did you tell me, Rose? Couldn't you have gone to Father O'Malley and confessed to him? Why did you have to tell *me*?"

"Because if the truth ever comes out, you'll be the one to help Rogan." She paused, "And he'll need your help."

Oliver rubbed his temples, tried to ease the sharp twinge that marked the beginnings of a headache. "Did you love my brother?"

"Love him? I loved him more than my life. You don't know how I tortured myself for years, wanting to tell him the truth about what I'd done. But how could I do that when it might destroy our happiness? I couldn't risk losing our family or the love we had for each other, so I kept silent." Those blue eyes met his, glistened. "If you're wondering whether we truly loved one another, I will swear on my children's lives that we did. When Gordon paid me a visit that last day and told me why he'd chosen my husband to dismantle and destroy, I wanted to tell Jonathan all about it, but I couldn't." Her voice cracked, split open. "And I'll never forgive myself for keeping silent."

"What does any of this have to do with Haywood?"

"He found his wife's personal journal." Rose sniffed, bit her lower lip. "She cared very much for her husband, had a child with him, and a life filled with every material possession she could imagine. But he was not the man who owned her heart. That man was her first love." Her voice wobbled, cracked, "That man was Jonathan."

Oliver stared at her. "His wife was Jonathan's old flame? Are you saying Haywood targeted him because the guy's wife admitted she'd never stopped loving my brother?"

Her lips quivered. "Yes, and if I hadn't interfered, they would have married, had their own children. Jonathan would still be alive."

"You don't know that. But…" The rest of the truth landed on his chest, stole his breath. "Elizabeth is their daughter."

She nodded. "That's why we have to make things right for Rogan and Elizabeth. I owe it to Jonathan."

The beginnings of Oliver's headache burst into a full-blown one. "It's going to be one big mess to try and convince them they belong together without revealing too much."

"I know." Her voice dipped, turned soft. "I was hoping you could help me."

He sighed. Why couldn't relationships ever be easy? Why did they always have to be untangled, interpreted, and reworked? "I've just got one more question, and I want you to shoot straight with me on this one."

Rose shook her head, her voice firm. "No, Oliver. Don't ask. Not now."

"When? You said you wanted me to protect Rogan. How can I do that if I don't know the whole story?" Did she think he *wanted* to know? Hell, he wished they'd never had this conversation, but he loved his nephew and he wouldn't see him hurt or blindsided.

"I'm not ready to reveal that pain." She laid a hand on his arm, gentled her voice, "But if I die before I've told you, the truth about Rogan's real father is in a lockbox at the bank. It's a single name in a yellow envelope, and no one but you will know its significance."

14

News of Rogan and Elizabeth's "uncoupling" crept through town, soft and quiet, like a secret that was doing it's damnedest not to be revealed. Tate heard about the split from his Aunt Camille, who'd deduced there was trouble when Elizabeth turned pale and stumbled through excuses as to why the couple hadn't been spotted together in days. And when Camille flat-out asked Rogan what was going on, he looked her in the eye and said, *No comment.*

Now if those weren't statements implying break-up and an unpleasant one, then Tate didn't know relationships. Unfortunately, he'd known his share and they usually ended in tears, accusations, and a flying object or two.

So, what *had* happened between the couple he'd have sworn was headed down the altar and a blissful life with kids, a picket fence, *and* a dog? Had Elizabeth broken down and confessed who she was and why she was in Reunion Gap? He rubbed his jaw, considered the possibility. She obviously loved the guy, so in that scenario, what would a person do? Tell the truth and risk losing him, or bury the truth and only reveal it if necessary, knowing the second option was sure disaster?

Tate had made a deal with Elizabeth that she'd keep her identity a secret until negotiations for the factory were complete. She'd done that, and the factory was set to open in a few days. Had love and a heavy conscience forced her to tell Rogan the truth? And what if Rogan proved as righteous and unbending as his father and refused to understand that, in this case, the means did justify the end? Would he really dump her? Pretend he didn't care, or if he did care, it didn't matter because the lie was too great? What a mess. Those two loved each other; that's all he'd heard about from his aunt and every other female in town since he'd gotten back. Some were jealous, others heartsick that they'd lost out on a chance with Rogan Donovan, but there were quite a few who were happy for the couple, said it proved that second chances and happily-ever-after still existed. Whatever the reason, he was going to find out tonight.

He entered JD Manufacturing, closed the door behind him. The place sure looked different from a few months ago. Organized, clean, bright, and filled with machinery. Rogan's father would be proud of him, but then Jonathan Donovan had been the kind of man to understand and appreciate hard work and integrity. Unlike Harrison Alexander, who only cared about results and besting his opponent in a world where *everyone* was his opponent, even his children. Tate made his way down the shop floor, took in the table saws and jointers that would begin manufacturing dressers, nightstands, and desks for HA Properties' hotels in a few days. It felt good to be JD Manufacturing's first order, symbolic in a victorious way over Harrison Alexander and his attempts to thwart the company. What better vengeance than to use the old man's company to pay retribution to the man he'd destroyed?

Tate found Rogan in his office, spreadsheets scattered in front of him, a beer near his right hand. "Figured I'd find you with your spreadsheets."

Rogan glanced up, squinted. "What are you doing here?"

"Checking up on you, what else?" He sank into the empty chair on the other side of the desk, took in the unshaven face, the bloodshot eyes, the wrinkled shirt. "What the hell happened to you? You look like crap."

The other man's gaze narrowed. "I've been busy."

"Uh-huh." He waited for Rogan to say more, but the guy clamped his mouth shut and shot him a look that said *ask again and you'll wish you hadn't*. Tate ignored the look and plowed on, "Does this have anything to do with Elizabeth? I thought I heard something about—"

"That's enough." The jaw twitched, the brackets around his mouth deepened. "We're not having that conversation."

"What conversation? Oh, you mean the one about you and Elizabeth?" Tate rubbed his jaw, nodded. "Fine. We don't have to talk about her, or why you look like you've been steamrolled. She's just a woman, right? Lots of other ones out there." He laughed. "We both know that, just like we know we can pretty much have our pick. Blondes, brunettes—"

"Shut up."

"But here's the thing. We don't want those other women, do we?"

Rogan Donovan looked like he wanted to fly across the desk and put a fist in Tate's face. "What would you know about relationships? A one-night stand isn't a relationship." He clenched his fists, ground out, "It's all a crap-shoot anyway. You think you know a person, you spit out the touchy-feely emotions and open up because that's how it works. And then you know what happens? It all goes to hell. You know why? Because she's been lying to you the whole time, telling you what she wants you to hear, hiding what she doesn't want you to know. And when you call her on it, what does she go and do? She friggin' cries and tells you she loves you. What the hell are you supposed to do with *that*?"

Tate cleared his throat. That was a hell of a lot of emotion from a guy who liked to play it cool. Whether he wanted to admit it or not, Rogan was in love with Elizabeth, and lies or not, he couldn't just fall out of love with her. It wasn't that simple. Tate should know. "I'm the last person who's qualified to give advice on relationships, but you look like you've been flattened and you sound like you're running out of oxygen. I've heard love does that to a guy, so I'm guessing you still love her. If the whispers going around town are half-true, she's as miserable as you are."

"Again, not open for discussion."

"If you say so." This wasn't the time to tell Rogan he knew Elizabeth's true identity, had known it for some time, and had persuaded her to remain silent. The man might not take too kindly to that bit of disclosure. In fact, it might earn Tate a black eye or a busted nose, so, no thank you. Yes, he'd admit what he'd done to protect him, and then he'd apologize for the subterfuge—just not tonight. "Okay, then." Tate stood, smoothed the creases from his slacks. "I guess I'll head out. Good luck with the opening."

"Hold on a second." Rogan pushed back his chair, stood. "Whatever happened with that guy you were going to investigate? Remember, the one your father wrote checks to with no backup information?"

Tate zeroed in on the paperweight sitting on the edge of Rogan's desk. *Play it cool. Don't give anything away until you find out what he knows. He could be fishing. Doesn't mean he knows Haywood is Elizabeth's father.* He rubbed his jaw, took his time answering. "Oh, yeah, I almost forgot about that guy. Dead end." Tate shook his head, dragged his gaze back to Rogan's. "Sorry."

Rogan crossed his arms over his chest, narrowed his gaze. "You were damn insistent when you brought the file to me. Don't tell me some bullshit about how you almost forgot about the guy. The Tate Alexander I knew didn't forget or give up on anything." Before Tate could respond, he said, "I think you know exactly who that man was and I think that's why you don't want to tell me."

Tate had bluffed his way through a lot of poker hands, and if he wanted to, he was fairly certain he could fool Rogan Donovan. But just because he could didn't mean he should. This was about a lot more than winning a pile of money at cards; this was about honor and doing the right thing. He blew out a long breath. "Yeah, I know all about the guy. Bastard," he mumbled under his breath.

"Yup, sounds about right."

"Look, I know I should have told you."

A scowl, followed by, "Right again."

"But I couldn't." Tate hesitated, reworked his thoughts. "How could I tell you the man who ruined your father's life was Elizabeth's father? I hated finding that out and I wanted to keep it from you as long as I could."

"Did she know you knew?"

Damn, this was not going the way he'd planned. If he weren't careful, he could still end up with a black eye and a broken nose before he left here tonight. He sighed. "She knew. I was the one who confronted her about it, made her promise not to tell you the truth until the deal was done and you'd agreed to let her help you. She didn't like that, said she couldn't stand not telling you and didn't want to wait that long. I boxed her in and didn't give her a choice. I didn't trust her." Pause. "Not when she said she was just trying to do right by your family, and not even when she said she loved you. Maybe I should have believed her; I don't know. I thought she might be playing you." Another sigh, this one louder, longer. "I told her I'd match whatever money she loaned you; the more money in the pot, the faster the project got completed."

"Why would you do that?"

"I might not be able to prove my old man was involved in this scheme, but his handprints are all over it. He owes you for everything he took from your family, and the few hundred thousand I dumped into your company is nothing compared to what he took."

Rogan moved toward him, stopped when he was a few feet away. "That's not what I was talking about." Those blues eyes turned to ice. "Why would you do that to Elizabeth?"

"Huh? I told you. I thought she was playing you."

"Damn you!" The left hook connected with Tate's nose in a sickening crack that doubled him over. "Stay away from her or next time, it'll be a lot worse than your nose."

ROGAN SAT on the front porch watching the sun set. Tomorrow JD Manufacturing opened its doors. Finally, his father's dream would be realized. He should have been elated, or at least relieved, that he'd honored his father's wishes.

But he was neither.

He sipped his beer, tried to ignore the mugginess clinging to his T-shirt. It was too damn hot to sit outside, but going indoors with the ceiling fans meant risking the inquisitive looks from his mother. He'd rather sweat. Besides, he had too much to think about.

It had been five days since he'd last seen Elizabeth. Six days since he learned he was going to be a father. *A father*. He still couldn't grasp the idea, or maybe what he couldn't grasp was having a kid without being with the mother. But here they were, split and pregnant. He'd have to talk to Elizabeth soon and get a game plan for this parenting gig. What was it going to look like? How would they manage it? Would he be one of those dads who let his kid have ice cream for breakfast, or would he deny him sugar?

He had no idea.

But then, he'd never thought he'd have to figure it out alone. Knowing Elizabeth, she'd have a manual of do's and don'ts, but that wasn't like having her in the same household, figuring out the kid together. And maybe that's why he hadn't called her yet. He was afraid of what he might say. *I forgive you. I want to spend the rest of my life with you.*

But could he ever trust her again?

Tate Alexander's visit the other night had confused and infuriated him to the point he'd punched him in the nose. If the guy tried a BS move like that again, Rogan would make sure he did a lot more than just bloody that damn nose. Maybe the guy was trying to protect Rogan, but he had no right to interfere with Elizabeth.

Would the outcome have been different if she'd come to him and divulged the truth?

Who could say?

Alexander could call it whatever fancy name suited him, but he'd blackmailed Elizabeth into *not* telling Rogan the truth. Damn the man. Rogan should have finished off with a second punch to the nose and broken it. Wonder what pretty boy told inquiring minds about the swollen nose? It wasn't hard to picture someone slugging the guy: jealous boyfriend, jealous ex-girlfriend…any number of choices.

At least Rogan's mother hadn't asked about Elizabeth lately, though she had taken to eagle-eyeing him whenever he walked into the room, as though she sensed the confusion in his soul and was attempting to pinpoint the size and location of it.

What the hell was he going to do?

Two beers later, he had no better handle on a plan of action than he had when he'd first learned of Elizabeth's duplicity. Oh, he'd calmed down, and he guessed he was taking a more rational approach to the mess, but he was so damn hurt. He'd *trusted* her and she'd lied to him.

And now she was pregnant.

Why hadn't they taken better precautions to *not* get pregnant? He had no idea.

But maybe he did. Maybe, deep down, he'd felt like he'd finally found the person he wanted in his life, and a child would complete that life. Or maybe he'd wanted her in his life so badly, he'd hoped she'd get pregnant. Could *that* be it? If so, how sick was that?

Rogan played with unplanned pregnancy scenarios and the psychological ramifications behind them through his third beer and the beginnings of a headache. Thankfully, his uncle drove up and stopped the madness and the headache.

Oliver hopped out of his van and waved. "I just left the shop. Thought you might be tending to some last-minute details. You all set for tomorrow?"

Rogan shrugged. "I'm as ready as I can be."

His uncle slid into the rocker next to him. "You'll be fine. Sure wish Jonathan could be here."

"I know."

"So...I hear you gave Tate Alexander a stay-the-hell-away-from-Elizabeth warning."

"Who told you that?"

He laughed. "Who else? Camille."

"Does she know everything that goes on in this town?"

"Pretty much. She's not too happy about what you did to that boy, said he's too handsome to have his face messed up by your temper."

"Right. And did that handsome face tell her why I punched him?"

Another laugh, this one deeper. "Probably not."

"Yeah, that's what I thought."

"Were you going to tell me about you and Elizabeth, or was I supposed to hear about it at the Cherry Top Diner?"

Rogan shrugged. "I guess I would have told you once I figured it out myself."

"Hmm."

"Yeah." They sat in the semidarkness, the crickets chirping around them, the scent of his mother's roses filling the air. It was like old times, and yet everything was different.

"She's Haywood's daughter."

"Wow. I'm sure you did not see that one coming."

Rogan stared straight ahead, pictured Elizabeth lying next to him… "Nope."

"Do you love her?"

"That's not really the point, is it?"

"Depends. Love can get through a lot, but you've got to have trust, too. She's broken it, so the question is, can you get it back? Or maybe the real question is, do you want to?"

"She's pregnant."

"Oh." Oliver paused, cleared his throat. "Now what?"

"Exactly."

"I'm not one to give advice, but don't let pride get in the way of being with the woman you love. Or fear. Men hate admitting they're afraid, but sometimes we're just chicken shits. Pride and fear will do you in every time."

Rogan slid him a look. "Are you speaking from experience?"

"Yup." He let out a quiet laugh. "But I'm working on it."

It was nice to know he wasn't the only screw-up in the relationship area. "So, how's it going?" Was he talking about someone in particular, say Jennifer Merrick?

"Too soon to tell, but there's hope."

"Ah. Hope. Interesting choice of words."

"We weren't talking about me. You only get so many chances,

Rogan." His voice turned rough. "If you love her and want to be with her, then tell her. Maybe get hitched, raise the baby, and add another few kids, plus a dog. You can never go wrong with a dog. What do you think?"

His uncle's words stayed with him the rest of the night and through the next day as Rogan stood on the shop floor while machines buzzed and whirred around him, honoring his father's hard work and dedication. But most of all, giving his father redemption. At some point, the whole town would know that Harrison Alexander had been involved in Jonathan Donovan's destruction, but not now, not until Rogan could confront the old man face-to-face and learn the *why*.

This day should have brought him peace and satisfaction, but it felt hollow, and he knew the reason. No matter what stories he told himself, life was not as vibrant without Elizabeth.

He needed her in his life, but could they start over?

Could they get their second chance?

There was only one way to find out.

Rogan stopped in the shop manager's office, told him he had an errand to run, and took off for the Peace & Harmony Inn. He raced up the front steps, placed his hand on the door handle, and hesitated. Since he and Elizabeth weren't technically together, he didn't know if Jennifer Merrick's invitation to enter without knocking still held. So, he knocked, waited.

When the door opened, Jennifer looked surprised to see him, maybe even shocked. "Rogan?"

"Mind if I come in?"

"Uh, sure." She stood aside to let him enter.

The sideways glance she gave him made him wonder how much she knew about his and Elizabeth's relationship. Probably more than he'd like, but at least she didn't have that ticked-and-going-to-make-you-pay-for-hurting-my-friend expression on her face. "Is Elizabeth here?"

Her eyes grew bright, her face pale. "No."

"I see." He hadn't anticipated that answer. "Do you know when she'll be back? If it's not too long, I could just hang out here." He remembered his manners, offered a smile. "If that's okay with you. Or if you know where she went…"

She shook her head, her eyes glistening with tears. "Oh, Rogan, I'm so sorry."

Sorry? Panic swirled through him. *Sorry for what?* "Where is she?"

Jennifer clasped her hands against her chest, said in a broken voice, "She's gone."

Rogan had lived through heartache and heartbreak, disappointment and disillusionment, but nothing compared to the pain surging through him at Jennifer's words. "Where'd she go?"

"Home."

The pain of that word burned a path from his soul to his chest, singed his brain. There'd been a time not long ago when he'd thought she might consider home Reunion Gap. Rogan opened his mouth to speak, but the words lodged in his throat, shut out sound.

Jennifer swiped at her eyes. "She waited for you to come. Every day, she waited, and you ignored her. Why would you do that? Don't you know how devastating it is for a woman to learn the man she loves, the man whose baby she's carrying, doesn't think enough of her to want to work things out?" The tears streamed down her cheeks, choked her words. "Why couldn't you have been different? Why did you have to be like every other man?"

He stepped back, tried to get away from the accusations that might be truer than he wanted to admit. "I had to think." Those words sounded feeble and empty right now. "She threw so much at me that I didn't know what was real and what was contrived. I

didn't know if I could ever trust her again, and I was hurting."
Hell yes, he'd been hurting. Bad.

"She was hurting, too," Jennifer said in a quiet voice.

"I see that now. Please, if you tell me where she is, I promise
I'll make it up to her." He sucked in a breath, forced out the truth,
"I love her."

The woman's dark gaze homed in on him, threatened to turn
him to ashes. "Do you love her enough to trust her again?"

"I do." He *had* to trust her; what was love without trust?

"And the baby? Children are a gift to the world and they
should be cherished and valued for who they are, not who we
want them to be." Her voice cracked. "Will you love your child,
no matter what?"

His own voice cracked. "No matter what."

"Then I'll tell you where she is."

ELIZABETH SET the sketch on the table, studied the piercing eyes,
the strong nose. Not that long ago, she hadn't known he existed.
She traced the firm lips, remembered how they felt against her
skin, thought of the words that flowed from them. Drawing faces
was not a skill she'd mastered, but re-creating Rogan's features
had come without thought or effort, as though the pencil came to
life and she was nothing more than the vessel through which it
delivered its mastery.

"Rogan," she whispered. "Why didn't you come for me?" Her
fingers followed the brackets around his mouth. "Why did you
give up on us?" A tear slipped down her cheek, landed on the
edge of the sketch. "Why did you give up on our baby?" More
tears, clogging her throat, blurring her vision. She loved him, and
she'd believed he loved her, too...enough to battle through all
manner of problems—even the lies she'd told.

But she should have known Rogan Donovan would not be able to find it in his heart to get past the lies, no matter how well intentioned they were. She'd broken his trust, a trust he didn't give often or easily. *That* had killed his love for her, and with it, their chances for a life together.

And their baby?

His refusal to acknowledge their child was all the answer she needed.

Rogan wasn't interested in being a father—at least not to their baby.

Elizabeth swiped at her tears, pressed her fingers against the outer corners of her eyes. Crying would not save her or heal her heart, and it certainly wouldn't help their child. Nothing would help now but her own resilience. Hadn't she learned long ago that those she loved didn't always love her? If her parents couldn't grant her unconditional love, why had she ever thought Rogan Donovan would?

She'd been a fool to trust in happiness and ever-after.

Elizabeth was a realist and from this day on, she'd do whatever was necessary for her child. She placed a hand on her belly, thought of the baby growing inside, innocent, pure. This child would know love, would know what it meant to belong, and would be encouraged to follow its own path, not the path chosen to please a parent.

Uncle Everett wanted her to remain here, had even suggested she move into his rambling home with the baby. Jennifer Merrick had offered her a place at the Peace & Harmony Inn where she'd help Elizabeth with the baby. *Giving back*, she'd called it. But the most surprising visit had come from Tate Alexander, the man who'd practically blackmailed her to remain quiet about her true identity. He'd apologized for his behavior, told her he was trying to protect a man he considered a friend. Then he'd smiled, touched his black-and-blue nose, and said the man hadn't appreciated the interference. Of course, that man was Rogan. Had he punched Tate? If so, why? She'd asked, but Tate Alexander didn't share secrets.

She'd come home to clear her head and put distance between the memories in Reunion Gap. If she stayed in her condo, she'd never risk seeing Rogan again, but what if she didn't want to live here? What if she wanted to take Jennifer up on her offer and move to Reunion Gap? It might be difficult, but eventually, she and Rogan would learn to ignore one another.

Wouldn't they?

Her chest ached at the thought of seeing him walking hand-in-hand along Main Street with another woman. Or holding a baby in his arms, one that wasn't theirs, the glint of a wedding band shining on his left finger.

How could she survive that?

This was not about her anymore. It was about doing whatever she had to in order to protect the baby. Elizabeth closed her eyes and sucked in a deep breath. *I will survive this. No matter what. I will survive, and I will be a good mother.*

"Elizabeth?"

Only one person's voice made her lightheaded. She inched her eyes open, stared. Rogan Donovan stood several feet away, looking tired and grim-faced, his gaze trained on hers. "What... what are you doing here?"

He moved toward her, his steps slow, cautious. "It seems I can't do things the normal way. I have to wait until you're hundreds of miles away to realize the truth." One step closer. When she didn't respond, he said, "Do you want to know what that is?"

She eyed him. "Do I?"

"I think so."

The hesitancy in his voice surprised her. "Okay, I'm listening."

Rogan closed the distance between them, stopped when he was a touch away. "How about I've been a rigid, unbending fool, who refused to understand the reasons you didn't tell me the truth? Or, how about I've been an idiot who should have thanked you for coming into my life? Or maybe, how about I've been a jerk who should never have walked out when you told me we were pregnant?"

"We?" She raised a brow. "Are you going to get stretch marks and morning sickness?"

He shrugged. "It's a figure of speech."

"I see."

He reached out, tucked a lock of hair behind her ear. "But maybe the biggest truth is that you live in my soul, Elizabeth Hayes. I love you. I'm sorry it took me this long to realize what that really meant, and if you give me another chance, I'll spend the rest of my life making it up to you." He placed a large hand on her belly. "I want this baby, and I want *us*."

She covered his hand with hers, held his gaze. "Do you trust me, Rogan?"

His smile answered her question. "Always." And then, "Can you forgive me for being such a jerk?"

She nodded. "Just don't shut me out like that again. Relation-ships are about finding ways to work through difficult times. If we're going to do this, we've got to be in it together."

"I know." He leaned toward her, brushed his lips over hers. "What would you say to a quickie wedding?"

"I'd say that sounds like a proposal."

Another kiss, this one deeper, longer, slower. "That's exactly what it is."

Elizabeth sighed. "Then I'd say it sounds perfect."

"Yeah." He released her, knelt down and kissed her belly. "You, me, and Baby Donovan. Now that's perfect."

15

Tate opened the newspaper and flipped to the business section. He scanned the financial section as he sipped his coffee and ate his breakfast. Astrid remembered how he liked his eggs, and since his sister wasn't around, he could enjoy his bacon without one of her raised-brow lectures. Knowing Meredith, she'd switched back and forth from vegetarian to meat three times since he'd last seen her. It was one thing to follow a lifestyle because you believed in it, but with his sister, it was usually more about following a trend. Interesting how neither of his siblings had visited the old man yet. If it had been their mother, they'd have been at her bedside the next morning.

Harrison Alexander might be able to buy businesses, votes, and some people, but he couldn't buy his own children, no matter what the incentive. They stuck together, despite their different lifestyles and beliefs, and the common denominator that was stronger than the blood that bound them, was their love for their deceased mother and their dislike for their tyrant father.

"Mr. Tate, would you like some fresh strawberries?" Astrid stood at the other end of the ridiculously long dining room table, hands folded over her ample middle. "They're very sweet."

How could he say no to strawberries and an honest smile? "Sure, but just a few. I'm not going to fit into my pants if I keep eating like this."

Her laugh swept along the table, swirled around him. "You will always be perfect, Mr. Tate."

He patted his flat belly, grinned. "I'll remember you said that."

Another laugh and a nod. "I'll be back in two minutes."

When she'd gone, Tate turned back to his paper and the last of his bacon. In all the years Astrid Longhouse worked for them, had his father ever had a conversation with her? Did he know her son attended the University of Pittsburgh and became a pharmacist? Or that her daughter lived in New Mexico? Doubtful. Harrison Alexander didn't care about anyone but those who served a purpose as a means to exercise power and control an outcome. Well, he couldn't control anything right now, and the doctors weren't sure if or when he might regain his faculties. The old man was out of the hospital, living in the east wing of the house with a full-time nurse and daily visits from all sorts of therapists. He still couldn't form a complete sentence, or remember, and struggled with judgment, which meant he wasn't taking over the company anytime soon…if ever.

That gave Tate time to continue his investigations into the company and try to ferret out the corruption that existed there. The case with Jonathan Donovan was only one of many, he was certain of it. Speaking of the Donovans, word in town was that Rogan and Elizabeth were getting hitched in two weeks, and there might be a reason for the hasty nuptials, though no one would admit there could be a Baby Donovan on the way.

Was that why Rogan's sister was in town? Camille had called him the second her niece rolled into Reunion Gap.

Guess who's back in town?

No idea.

My niece. Pause. *Charlotte. You know, long auburn hair, green eyes, leggy.*

Yeah, he knew all right. *And?* His pulse had skipped three beats when he heard Charlotte's name.

And nothing. Just thought you'd like to know. I'm having lunch with her tomorrow at The Oak Table. Her laughter had filled the phone line. *Which means we should finish around 2:00 p.m. and who's to say you couldn't be walking by at that exact moment? If you were interested, I mean...*

They both knew he'd been interested for years and was doing his damnedest to hide it, even from himself. *Thanks.*

Camille would make a great investigator if she ever decided on that line of work. Her calculations regarding her niece's departure from the restaurant were damn near perfect. At 2:08 p.m., Charlotte left The Oak Table. Alone.

Tate got out of his car and moved toward her, his long strides catching her before she reached the sporty coupe he assumed was hers. "Hello, Charlotte."

Charlotte Donovan swung around, her auburn curls swirling about her shoulders, an expression that could only be called horror on her face. "Tate?"

He forced a smile, tried to remain calm when he was anything *but* calm. His gaze drifted to her lips, remembered the taste of them...

"Stop it." Those green eyes narrowed on him as if she were trying to decide whether to lunge at him or turn and run.

She could deny the electricity between them all she wanted, but three seconds in the same room and *zap*, the pull was too strong to resist. They'd pretended they didn't recognize it for what it was—pure, hot need—and had done a good job of it until one night in Chicago five months ago. Maybe it was the tequila, or maybe it was the fact that they were hundreds of miles from

Reunion Gap and nobody knew the history between the Alexanders and the Donovans.

Or maybe it was simply destiny playing her long-overdue hand.

Who could say?

Let her try to deny that night. There'd been so much damn passion flowing between them, the first kiss jolted them as if they'd been struck by lightning. The second stole their speech, their breath...their common sense. Alexanders should not mix with Donovans, but Tate and Charlotte ignored the rules, and when they touched, their world spun out of control.

"I said stop it."

Tate blinked and pushed images of a naked Charlotte Donovan from his brain. What he wouldn't give for another night with her... But that wasn't going to happen, not now anyway because he'd screwed up and they both knew it. He pretended nonchalance, as though he wouldn't give half his fortune to be with her again. "I'm not doing anything." Tate moved closer, worked up a smile. "Do you want me to? Is that why you're so cranky?"

Those full lips stretched into a thin line. "I'd rather spend the night with a toad than with you."

She was so damn beautiful. How could he look at her and not think about every inch of that delectable body...every minute of that night? "Are you thinking about what happened in Chicago?" He rubbed his jaw, studied her. "I am." His gaze shot to the slender neck, slid to the opening of her blouse. "I can't look at a chocolate lava cake without wanting a taste." His voice dipped. "And one taste is never enough, is it?" He still remembered the need in her voice when she said, *I want you, again, Tate. Once will never be enough.*

"You're no gentleman."

Now she was annoying him. Could she not admit what had happened in Chicago, maybe admit she wanted it to happen again? He wouldn't let her see how her words hurt him, but they cut deep. After their night together, he'd awakened to an empty bed. No note, no "see you later." Nothing but a few long strands of auburn hair on the pillow next to him and a hole in his heart. Sure, he could have called her mother and asked for Charlotte's phone number, but he was pretty sure Charlotte wouldn't want that. And he wasn't going to ask Rogan. In retrospect, he should have made the damn phone calls and taken the consequences. But he hadn't and Charlotte Donovan had plagued him, the image of her in his bed burned in his brain.

That killed the chance of another woman sharing his bed, and that had become a problem—a big one. "Look," he said, deciding honesty was his best shot with this woman. "I wanted to call you…I just didn't think I should call your mother and I sure as hell wasn't about to contact Rogan." He sighed, dragged a hand through his hair. "I thought maybe if I let enough time go by, I'd realize whatever happened that night was more about the tequila and not a real attraction." Another sigh. "At least I hoped to hell that's what it was." She stood very still, lips pinched. "But, I should have known better." He moved closer, placed his hands on her shoulders. "I think whatever happened between us could be real, and I think we owe it to ourselves to find out."

The pinched lips and dagger-shooting gaze said she was preparing for a comeback and it was going to be a missile. "Go to hell. You had months to get in touch with me, and don't give me that story about not wanting my mother and brother to find out. We both know you had no intention of seeing me again, so save the story for some starry-eyed groupie who believes you, because I don't."

Tate opened his mouth to speak. *I'm sorry I hurt you. Give me another chance, let me show you I care. Please.* He tried to force out the apology and the promise, but fear stopped him, held his tongue.

Maybe she really did hate him.

Charlotte scowled. "Yeah, that's exactly what I thought. The big player has no plays. You know, you gave a very nice speech about owing it to ourselves to find out if what happened is real, but please, don't repeat it." Her voice chilled him. "Jason wouldn't be impressed."

"Jason?" *Who the hell was Jason?*

"My boyfriend. He'll be here in a few days." And with that she turned, head held high, and walked away.

The End

IN CASE YOU'RE WONDERING...

Now that you've finished *Strangers Like Us*, I hope you're wondering about a few of the residents and what happens next. Of course, you've figured out the second story in this series is about Tate Alexander and Charlotte Donovan. In *Liars Like Us*, you'll learn what happened to make Charlotte "detest" Tate...but does she really? And what could Tate possibly do to change her mind so she'll give him a second chance? I've got a few ideas...

Do you also want to know more about Hope Merrick? There's a reason you haven't officially "met" her yet, but you will in *Liars Like Us*. I have a soft spot for a struggling child, so stay tuned. Speaking of Hope, what about her mother and Oliver? Are they going to get together? And when is Jennifer going to actually visit her mother? The answers are coming...

I can't wait to put Carter and Camille Alexander on the same page so you can watch them interact. What a womanizer! Why is Camille still hanging onto a doomed marriage and a loser husband? Beyond the obvious of money and power...could she really *love* the jerk? We'll find out.

Who's Rogan's real father? Unlike *A Family Affair*, I do know the real father, and you will too...*eventually*.

And last, but certainly not least, there's Harrison Alexander. That horrid man has been talked about quite a bit, but you haven't officially met him. You'll have an opportunity to do so if he can recover enough from his stroke to speak…

I'm not saying you'll discover everything I've mentioned above in *Liars Like Us*. Some answers might not come until the third book, *Lovers Like Us*…or the one after that. Either way, it's going to get very interesting. And if you're familiar with my books, you know they're not complete without a secret journal or two!

Guess we'll have to wait and see what happens!

Many thanks for choosing to spend your time reading *Strangers Like Us*. If you enjoyed it, please consider writing a review on the site where you purchased it.

If you'd like to be notified of my new releases, please sign up at http://www.marycampisi.com

ABOUT THE AUTHOR

Mary Campisi writes emotion-packed books about second chances. Whether contemporary romances, women's fiction, or Regency historicals, her books all center on belief in the beauty of that second chance. Her small town romances center around family life, friendship, and forgiveness as they explore the issues of today's contemporary women.

Mary should have known she'd become a writer when at age thirteen she began changing the ending to all the books she read. It took several years and a number of jobs, including registered nurse, receptionist in a swanky hair salon, accounts payable clerk, and practice manager in an OB/GYN office, for her to rediscover writing. Enter a mouse-less computer, a floppy disk, and a dream large enough to fill a zip drive. The rest of the story lives on in every book she writes.

When she's not working on her craft or following the lives of five adult children, Mary's digging in the dirt with her flowers and herbs, cooking, reading, walking her rescue lab mix, Cooper, or, on the perfect day, riding off into the sunset with her very own hero/husband on his Harley Ultra Limited.

If you would like to be notified when Mary has a new release, please sign up at http://www.marycampisi.com/newsletter.

To learn more about Mary and her books…

https://www.marycampisi.com

mary@marycampisi.com

OTHER BOOKS BY MARY CAMPISI

Contemporary Romance:

Truth in Lies Series

Book One: *A Family Affair*

Book Two: *A Family Affair: Spring*

Book Three: *A Family Affair: Summer*

Book Four: *A Family Affair: Fall*

Book Five: *A Family Affair: Christmas*

Book Six: *A Family Affair: Winter*

Book Seven: *A Family Affair: The Promise*

Book Eight: *A Family Affair: The Secret*

Book Nine: *A Family Affair: The Wish*

Book Ten: *A Family Affair: The Gift*

Book Eleven: *A Family Affair: The Weddings, a novella*

Book Twelve: *A Family Affair: The Cabin, a novella*

Book Thirteen: *A Family Affair: The Return*

NEW: Reunion Gap Series

Book One: *Strangers Like Us*

Book Two: *Liars Like Us*

Book Three: *Lovers Like Us*

More to come…

That Second Chance Series

Book One: *Pulling Home*

Book Two: *The Way They Were*

Book Three: *Simple Riches*

Book Four: *Paradise Found*

Book Five: *Not Your Everyday Housewife*

Book Six: *The Butterfly Garden*

That Second Chance Boxed Set 1-3

That Second Chance Boxed Set 4-6

That Second Chance Complete Boxed Set 1-6

The Betrayed Trilogy

Book One: *Pieces of You*

Book Two: *Secrets of You*

Book Three: *What's Left of Her*: a novella

The Betrayed Trilogy Boxed Set

Begin Again

The Sweetest Deal

Regency Historical:

An Unlikely Husband Series

Book One - *The Seduction of Sophie Seacrest*

Book Two - *A Taste of Seduction*

Book Three - *A Touch of Seduction*, a novella

Book Four - *A Scent of Seduction*

An Unlikely Husband Boxed Set

The Model Wife Series

Book One: *The Redemption of Madeline Munrove*

Young Adult:

Pretending Normal

CPSIA information can be obtained
at www.ICGtesting.com
Printed in the USA
LVOW03s0341270717
542797LV00001B/156/P